AMELIA

Going Under Rising to the Top

Belle Blaney

Published by: Soul True Self Productions.

Printed in the United State of America.

Cover Designed by: Iram Shahzadi

Author photograph by: Chris A. Cherbas

Editing by Jule Blakeley Monnens

This book is dedicated to

Sheila O'Connell Roussell –

who's Irish story contributions have made Amelia

all the more richer and endearing to my heritage.

Prologue
Amelia

She ran faster than she'd run the past few nights. The moon had crested and the evening's last light hit the narrow path that lied ahead. Amelia wasn't a runner or even an athlete of her younger days. In fact, she'd only started this twilight ritual a week ago. It wasn't exercising.

Amelia ran so that she would not dissolve. She ran to plan her escape.

At age 50, she had lost her parents prematurely, at the hands of a life *less-lived*. Her husband had left her without warning, and the one person that understood her best, died from a broken heart. She was running from a life of secrets, and unwanted changes cruelly thrust upon her.

When she finally stopped running, blackness surrounded her, and she tried to remember how long she'd been out. In sudden clarity, she was confident that this would be the last run. She didn't know how, but she would survive this. It meant she would need to do something different to battle this grief and loneliness.

As she sat on the park bench, pondering this shift, her thoughts wandered to her granddaughter, Franki. She wondered if perhaps her losses could be Franki's gain and that whatever would come next, she would have a chance at a different experience of family.

Amelia walked herself back home with resolve. She would begin by writing down her story, telling of the events leading to her heartbreak, and if the time were ever right, Franki would read it, and she would know her grandmother, and Amelia could be healed.

RIDING THE WAVE

No trumpets sound when the important decision of
our life are made.
~Agnes De Mille

9

1

1967

Our family never went anywhere except to church and the Pacific Ocean a few hours away. Our lives centered on being Irish, seemingly good and frugal. Our home contained furnishings from the Goodwill but only things Mom could justify as looking Irish.

"Oh, look. This step stool looks like it belonged at my great grandfather's potato farm!" Mom might say. Anyone could see that it was just an old Ethan Allen wooden stool, but it made her happy to envision it in a barn somewhere in rural Ireland, next to potato-sacks. My clothes were hand-me-downs from Marissa Myers, two years older, 3 inches taller and 10 pounds heavier. I looked like a freak most of the time, except in the summer at the beach. There I didn't mind wearing baggy pedal-pushers since I was barefoot most of the time anyway.

Those trips to the Washington coast were my favorite time of year, and I looked forward to them each summer. We stayed with Grandpa Frank and Grandma Jane (my namesake) at their beach resort. Mom would laugh every time someone referred to the place as a resort because it was nothing more than six individual run-down cabins with old furniture and rusted metal.

My family of eight, sometimes took one of the cabins for our lodging, but my favorite was when I was allowed to sleep in the loft above the kitchen in the main house. The loft was accessible by a vertical wooden ladder and once on top, there was barely enough room for me to stand. I liked to peek down, as if spying, on Grandma Jane as she cooked our breakfast or chatted with Mom at the kitchen table. She always had homemade baked bread that tasted like heaven. Mom contribute by bringing her freezer strawberry jam and real butter.

There were always eggs, which I hated as a child but as the only girl, I could usually exempt myself from having to eat eggs and often won the second piece of toast and jam with my *"pretty-please"* and girlish smile. Life at Grandma Jane's was perfect.

During the day, we played on the beach hunting sand dollars delivered by the tide or digging clams for Grandma's famous chowder. These summer memories carried me through the long drizzly rain season that followed. The Pacific Northwest was a beautiful place to live, but most of its inhabitants have webbed feet and water repelling skin.

When Dad announced we were going to take a vacation to Disney Land in California, instead of our usual, I was skeptical, primarily because the real purpose was to attend a church revival, and going to church anywhere was equal to swallowing a teaspoon of cod liver oil. Still, perhaps I could endure this religious-pain in exchange for a bit of California sun.

Dad was a protestant preacher, and in my home that meant three things: we were at church every time the doors were open, the home was filled with moral coding — I didn't realize that soap didn't go in the mouth until I was 15 — and there was a constant stream of "Christians" entertained for dinner or bible study. The house was never quiet, and I didn't like the way some visitors smelled or how they glared at me. I didn't appreciate the need to be a good Christian, and I didn't *get* half of the Christian rules like not drinking wine. Didn't Jesus drink wine? Dad explained that being drunk with wine was the sin and so *why play with fate*? *"Do not drink at all,"* he'd say. This was illogical and unnecessary thinking.

On the day of our departure to California, the first of many sibling squabbles broke out. Who got to sit by a window, who farted? Screams that someone's leg touched another's and on and on. Having to share the station wagon with five brothers for the long three-day drive to California was regrettably the price to pay for the promise of warm ocean water and white-hot sand — where the sun never slept and people didn't need to own umbrellas.

We started out early on June 15th, traveling down the coastal highway through Washington and then Oregon, often catching a glimpse of the Pacific Ocean. On our second morning out, we stopped at Denny's restaurant for a huge breakfast; kids ate for 99 cents, which Dad continually boasted about because *saving was a virtue*.

That afternoon, back on the road, Mom included a story that she often repeated and was often requested. The story was of an Irish ancestor that lived in Northern Ireland with added details like a family castle, now in ruins. The O'Malley's & Blayney's were farmers in

Ireland, until around the 1800s, when they immigrated to Canada. We all loved to hear the stories of life in Ireland, and Mom would muster up her borrowed Irish accent when it was especially important to understand the significance of the characters.

We arrived at Uncle Michael's and Aunt Vanessa's on a Saturday, the evening of our third day. Uncle Michael was Mom's brother and a successful businessman. Their home was entirely unlike ours. There was not one piece of furniture that was from the Goodwill, and Uncle Michael dressed in well-fitted business suits even at the breakfast table! The room I stayed in had a fancy canopy bed with its own bathroom and my brothers doubled up in another two bedrooms with Mom and Dad in the master suite.

Uncle Michael and Aunt Vanessa slept in their colossal travel trailer parked alongside their house during our time there.

Aunt Vanessa said it was a treat for them to stay out in the motorhome, so we weren't to feel that our visit had inconvenienced anyone. They were delighted we'd come for a visit.

On Sunday, a day after our arrival, we drove a short distance to a local Protestant church that had a large white tent in the parking lot. Inside the tent were rows of metal chairs facing a staging area, where, I imagined, all the Christian rules would be preached. I survived the four days of people carrying-on, crying, and loud exaggerated preaching by drawing pictures on the revival-bulletin (which laid out all the fun we were to have over the next few days). The collection of money seemed to be the most critical part of the service, and if you didn't put your money in the basket, you were stared at so, of course, it was in your best interest to drop your coins into the basket with as much noise as possible.

There was a different preacher every night, and on Tuesday, it was Dad's turn. All of the family sat in the front row because that is what the preacher's family did. I hated this most of all.

At the revival, Dad preached louder and more animated than back home. I guess it was because he was expected to. I just know I was glad when the week of jumping up and down and being saved was over.

Before going to Disney World, we made a plan to spend a day at the beach. I had a new bathing suit from Woolworths and sandals from St. Vincent Thrift Store. Mom liked to buy our clothes at second-hand stores saying there was no need for new clothes when used were perfectly fine, and she sometimes reminded us how miserably poor our Irish ancestors were before immigrating to Canada.

She tried this tactic out one day during dinner. When I was around ten years old, Mom had been on a health-kick after reading books by Adele Davis. Every Wednesday we had beef-liver because Adele said it was good for us. The liver was not good; Adele was wrong. Still, every Wednesday, Mom served it as our family dinner. Except for Samuel, the youngest boy, who didn't seem to mind, the rest of us picked at the awful slab of liver while sitting a very long time at the dinner table. "You will sit there until you eat it!" Mom scolded.

One Wednesday, liver presented, brother Nathanial moaned as his plate was placed in front of him. His disapproving groans irritated Mom.

"Nathanial, you should be thankful we have food! Think of those starving children back in Tyrone who only had a few potatoes to eat!" We had heard this line many times. The table grew quiet. Finally, Nathanial grunted back at Mom, "Name Two!"

Mom's face got red as she turned and walked away and we all giggled. The only way to get out of eating the liver was to either cut it up and feed it secretly to the dog (and even the dog could take so much) or to throw it up. If we threw up or even gagged, we were sent straight to our rooms without dinner. Mom thought this was punishment, but it was really a blessing. The liver-campaign only last for a few months.

I had never seen the California ocean but I had seen postcards from Aunt Mary. Aunt Mary was not really our Aunt but a cousin. We called her our Aunt because she was much older than a cousin should be, I guess. Anyway, Aunt Mary lived in California and dressed like a movie star. She wore bright red lipstick with pancake makeup and enough mascara that I wondered how she opened her eyes. One of the postcards, Aunt Mary sent us, included one of the Pacific Ocean at Long Beach, California. I secretly hoped that the postcard pictures of the beautiful California beaches were exactly like it really looked, not altered as profoundly as Aunt Mary's face.

I was not disappointed. There it was — endless white sand and ocean so postcard-blue. After setting up our towels, ice chest filled with Shasta soda pop, and an umbrella for shade, I led the run to the water's edge. My brothers were bigger than me but not faster and not as brave. I hit the water with determination and force. Mom yelled at us to not go out too far, but I knew what I was doing. I'd dreamt of this moment all the way down the coast, and I wasn't about to slow down now.

Nathanial had a styrofoam body board and he let me try it out first. We wadded out against each incoming wave and rode that wave back toward shore before jumping off and going out again. Over and over , taking turns on the board or merely body-surfing; I was certain this would be the best day of my life.

The sun was bright, and the sounds of the ocean loomed large in stereo. Braver and braver, we went further out until the sound of Mom's protests were muffled and beyond understanding. As I looked back toward shore, I saw her standing there waving both arms in the air. Even for Mom, this seemed a little over the top. Looking around, I didn't see Nathanial or any of my brothers. Then a massive wave slapped my back and sent me head first into the water. The current was whipping my slender 12-year-old body deeper under the current then dragging me back out to sea. The water surface was out of reach, but I could still see the bright sun above. My heart pounded as I realized I had lost control of the ability to get back to the surface . My head felt dizzy.

Suddenly, the water changed and the sun was no longer visible as I was looking up. Instead, the surface looked like a solid sheet of ice and beyond that, darkness. The water grew colder and colder — darker and darker. The sounds of the ocean quieted, and the water became still. No longer dizzy, my only thought was that I might not ever see Mom again.

I floated downward, making no sense of what was happening. Swirls of something brown surrounded me. I could make out large sunflowers against the dark background.

What? My bathing suit was pink! I searched my brain to make sense of it. My feet felt heavy like when I wore galoshes walking through thick mud puddles. None of this made sense!

Then, I heard someone talking — no, someone talking in my head. With no other sounds audible, the voice was clear.

"Fanny, are you sure? The water 'tis now warm and the sun bright with hope. Are you sure?"

I was thinking, as the voice spoke, that the water was *not* warm and there was only darkness. But, then again;

"I want to live! 'Twill be alright. Mary Ann 'twont understand. No, No! I want to live!" Ma, help me! Amelia, I'm scared.

In that instant, an arm pulled me from the water, drugged me to land and onto the hot California sand — and then all went black again.

2

The Other

"Amelia, can you hear me? Open your eyes sweet girl." Slowly, I opened my eyes to see Mom's face inches from my own. She was smiling and stroking my head as she had done so many times before when I was ill. "Amelia," she said, "You're back. We were all so worried." As I looked around the room, it left little doubt that I was in a hospital, and I was instantly aware how uncomfortable the bed was.

"Mom, where is everyone? Where's Dad and Nathanial?"

Again with a smile, "Your dad is right outside the door on the phone with Uncle Michael. The boys are at his house waiting to hear that you're ok".

"What happened? Why am I here?" I fussed.

"You had a little accident in the water, but you'll be ok, Amelia." With that guarded piece of information, I remembered my time under water.

"Did they find the other girl?" I asked.

"Other girl? No, Amelia, you were the only one out there. Now, try to rest. We will be right here."

Over the next few days, I heard the story repeated about the lifeguard that dove in looking for me, finally pulling me to the surface then swimming to shore. I heard about the way Mom was crying through the rescue attempts, and how Nathanial was kicking the sand in a fury, taking the blame for losing me in the waves. There was an ambulance, sirens and a bunch of people standing around to see what was going on. Dad said I was unconscious but kept muttering, "*I want to live.*" I had no memory of anything except the voices in my head when I was in the icy dark waters.

Where did I go that the water was so cold and the sun went away? Who is Fanny and why was she mentioning my name?

I spent two more days in the hospital. Being in the hospital was not that bad. I got lots of ice cream, and my brothers were nice to me. Nathanial was always nice, but sometimes James and Jack teased me until I cried. I didn't like to complain and tried not to, but when they called me *fish-eyes*, (because my eyes were bigger than my head and protruded when seen from the side) I usually gave in and ran off crying while they laughed. They also teased me about my wild hair, but that didn't make me cry because I liked my hair…it was like Mom's hair. Now, they were all sweet to me. Jack brought me a stuffed seal toy, and the twins returned with seashells from the beach. James Jr. didn't make this trip with us. He was already living on his own and playing at being an adult. But, he called every night to see how I was.

My dreams, when I slept, were of my time in the water. I never thought of the dreams as nightmares. I woke up thinking about the images — dark pools, the voices in my head and the swirls of brown fabric. It didn't make sense to feel so calm. I didn't tell anyone about the recurring dreams. I knew they would either worry about me, or they would think I was crazy. I preferred to avoid both.

When I was released, we went to Knott's Berry Farm and Disney World as planned. I grew tired more easily and sat on the park benches watching the boys take on the roller-coaster rides, but I still had a great time. I asked to go back to the ocean, just one more time, but parents can be overly cautious, and they vetoed my request. "Not this time, Amelia. My heart can't take it," was Mom's response.

"The ocean will be there for our next trip down here," was Dad's logic. I didn't fight it. Somehow, I knew they were right, and there needed to be space between my next adventure on the California coastal waters.

Five days after my near drowning, we were all sitting at another Denny's restaurant, and having another inexpensive breakfast as we started for home. We were all much quieter than usual. I broke the silence and asked, "Dad, do we know anyone named Fanny?" He smiled like a parent smiles when you've been sick and now feeling better.

"I can't think of anyone by that name. It's a funny name, isn't it? Why do you ask?"

Not answering his question, I continued with my own. "Was there another little girl in the water when I was out there?" His response was immediate.

"No, there was no one else there except the lifeguard looking for you." At this he was looking at me strangely, so I changed the subject by commenting how tasty my waffle was, and what a grand bargain we were getting for just under a dollar.

We left Los Angeles on a typically sunny California day with cooler than average temperature. It had been deliciously warm during our last few days with Uncle Michael. I didn't want to go back home to the rain and colder weather of the Pacific Northwest. I had considered asking if I could stay with my Aunt and Uncle. The California life seemed to fit me. Still, leaving Mom, Dad and brothers would be tough — but not impossible.

The crowded station wagon was still the downside of this California vacation — elbows bumping, cries erupting into; "stop touching me!" When it was my turn to sit by the window, I tuned out all sibling -madness, stare out at the swiftly passing scenery and muse about life as a grown up. With each passing beach house, I imagined living there alone.

As I was on one of these mind adventures, my memory returned to the dark waters. *"I want to live, Ma, help me"*.

Over and over, these words pounded in my head. Then a recalled memory. While I was slowly sinking deeper into the depths, I saw the brown swirl of fabric all around me as high up as my shoulders. At the time, I thought it was a blanket or something like that, but now I remembered its details — sunflowers!

I closed my eyes and tried to remember what it felt like having this material surround me. As I began to return to the car-chaos, Jack, nudged me. "Wake up princess. Are you deaf? Mom asked you a question." Back to reality, I wondered if it was too late to ask Uncle Michael to adopt me.

Food always tastes better when eaten outside, especially when on a picnic. Mom and Dad splurged, buying us restaurant fried chicken, creamed corn, mashed potatoes with gravy and extra biscuits. Sitting in the Redwood Forest, we ate as if we had forgotten all about the bargain-breakfast eaten just four hours ago. Our conversation was lively and mostly about which Disney ride was the best.

Dad broke in, "Amelia, I've been thinking about your question."

"What question?"

"The one about knowing someone named Fanny." Turning to Mom, he asked, "Honey, wasn't your grandmother's name Frances? Fanny was a popular nickname for Frances back then, right?"

Mom nodded as if to confirm his memory. "Ask your Grandma Jane when we get home. She'll remember."

Slow to respond, I finally asked, "Were there other relatives named Mary Ann or someone with my name?"

Mom eagerly chimed in. "Oh, Jim, remember when I was pregnant with Samuel and I did all that ancestry research?" He nodded in affirmation as he stuffed half a biscuit with jam in his mouth. "Well, I'll try to find my old notes, but I think there was a Mary Ann, and I think it was Frances' sister. I got your name,

Amelia, from my research because I thought it was so pretty. We'll look it up at home. Ok?"

I smiled and eagerly agreed it was a good idea. The table grew silent but only for a moment. Then Paddy, one of the twins, threw his chicken bone at Nathanial, missed, and hit me in the head hard enough to lodge the bone in my hair. Hysterical laughter erupted and out of an unconscious place I shouted, "Oh Chad, that was so funny!"

In unison, my brothers reacted, "Who's Chad?"

3

The Prize

Being from a sizable American-Irish family had its perks. My friend, Sarah, was an only child so visiting her house was quiet and normal. She had no idea what ethnicity she was and claimed we are all mutts anyway. If I said that to Mom, I would get the taste of Ivory soap in double dose. My family took great pride in our Irish roots, and so many of the stories around our dinner table were of our ancestors back in Ireland.

Dad was born James Patrick Nolan. He told us that the Nolans' were royalty of the Kings of Leinster and the Prince of the Foherta, Baron of Forth. He reminded us that the Nolan family - line was well known, to this day, in Ireland. We had memorized these Kings, Princes and Baron names because it was important to our parents, otherwise, we had no idea what these elitists meant to our American lives.

Mom was born Voada Marie O'Malley. Her dad was German, with an equally German name of William Franklin Bauer, nicknamed Frank. Even though Mom was half German, Grandma Jane ingrained the importance of securing her Irish roots by keeping the O'Malley name, even on her birth certificate. The story is told that Grandpa Frank wanted Mom's name to be Hilda, but Grandma insisted it be Irish. The compromise was Mom's middle name, Marie, after Grandpa's mother. I have been told several times, "keep the O'Malley name, Amelia. It is your roots and the very core of who you are."

On my birth certificate, I am *Amelia Jane O'Malley Nolan*. I was born last of the Nolan clan,; a delightful surprise after six male births.

So, here's the lineup of the O'Malley-Nolan children:

James, Jr.	Nathanial
Stephen	Samuel
Patrick "Paddy"	…and Me
Jack	

James was my senior by 14 years. He was a responsible boy, but tried to detach himself from personal tie to his younger siblings. Stephen and Paddy, were twins and inseparable. They finish each other's sentences and took the blame for the other, if punishment was foreseen.

Jack was the middle child, quiet and reserved. He lived in the shadows of his older siblings and benign to his younger brothers. He was easy going and agreeable. His natural ability to tune us all out was unnerving at times.

Samuel was the baby boy and just 18 months older than I. We shared some things, like books, because of our similar age, but I was smarter and more driven.

Nathaniel was my favorite. I don't know exactly how that happened, but it began, according to household legend, when I was born. Nathanial, age 3, jumped up and down when I was introduced as his little sister. From that day forward, he took an interest in me, and I bonded with him. Even though we were born in the same family, Nathanial and I were very different in personality. Nathanial was creative and spontaneous while I was analytical and liked things done in a certain way. We complemented each other and smoothed out our rough edges.

Nathanial protected me, and I kept him out of trouble. Once after school, the Stern brothers, Mac and Miles — bullies personified, caught up with us as we walked home. Mack started teasing me about my thick, wavy hair.

"Hey, witch! Wanna cast a spell on me?" Mack chided. Nathanial warned him to stop, but that just made the brothers angry, and the bullying got worse.

"Oh, that's right, fag. You probably wish you had that girly hair," said the younger Stern. Ignoring that strange comment, I turned to walk away pulling Nathaniel's sleeve.

From the back, Miles poked my head and laughed. "Look, her head's in there somewhere! Right, O'Smelly?"

Nathanial's eyes grew dark, and his hands drew up into a fist. Before I could stop him, he pivoted back around, and that fist caught Miles right in the jaw. Down he went, as Nathanial jumped on top of him, hitting him in the stomach.

Mack was screaming, "Get off of him!" But did nothing to help his brother.

Suddenly, Nathanial got up, brushed off his denim and said: "Next time, I won't go so easy on you." At that, he took my arm, and we walked away from the scene. I didn't know why the Stern brothers didn't follow us, but they never bother me again.

In school, Nathanial doodled…a lot! In our family, going to college was expected. My role, in our sibling-duo, was to make sure Nathanial passed all his classes. Even though Nathanial was two years ahead of me in school, I helped him with his homework and studying for exams, even in the advanced work.

Nathanial made sure I didn't take life too seriously. He pulled me out of my head and showed me how to have fun. This was how we teamed up — like Batman and Robin, we boosted. Mom warned me that once Nathanial hit high school, I should prepare myself for things to change. He would spend more time with his friends, she warned. I wasn't worried, as long as Nathanial had calculus or English literature, he would need me.

When we returned from our California trip, I had all but forgotten about the water incident. Ignoring the hard things in life was a personality trait that would both serve and harm me during my lifetime. I went on with my 12-year-old life of crossword puzzles, reading biographies of famous presidents and trying different chemicals to tame my wild hair.

On Sundays … every Sunday! … we went to Grandma Jane's for dinner after church. She had moved back from the coast after Grandpa Frank died, selling the resort. There was always an Irish-focused story told at the table that I looked forward to the most. Usually, the stories were about events vaguely mentioning specific people. On one particular Sunday though, Grandma Jane told a story about one specific ancestor named, Chadwallder

Blayney. Chad was the brother of Frances Jane — my great grandmother.

And there it was. *Frances.* Before Grandma Jane could continue her story, I rushed in and asked, "Grandma, was Frances called Fanny?"

Her reply was simply, "Yes," as if it was common knowledge. I continued,

"Did she have other siblings? Sisters?"

"Yes, Amelia and one of those sisters is your namesake, isn't that right, Voada?" Mom nodded and smiled sweetly at me.

"And, Grandma, was another sister named Mary Ann?"

"Mary Ann? Yes, Amelia. How did you know that?" I was silent as my mind raced back to last summer in the waters and the voices. It had been six months ago since we returned from the coastal trip. Mom's promise to look up her ancestors had faded with time, and the redwood forest picnic table conversation forgotten. Now, however, it was front and center.

"That's right, Amelia, I was going to find my research and tell you about your great-grandmother, Fanny. We'll still need to do that someday soon." I nodded as I lowered my head toward the roast pork and cabbage.

Grandma Jane continued with her story. "Chad was Frances' favorite brother. She would tell me about their adventures, how different they were in personality yet they took care of the each other. Chad was artsy while Fanny was the level-headed one who preferred studying the patterns of ant trails.

"Anyway, this story is about Chadwallder. They were very poor, so there was no money for art supplies, yet Chad could always make art out of twigs and grass. His father, Oliver Blayney, was a farmer and Jack of all Trades. He'd take the boys; Chad, Loulis, and Cian with him on the odd jobs necessary to feed the family. One day, a job took them into Ottawa where Oliver was to fix a thresher for a local farmer. Chad was the oldest of the boys, so his father told him to watch the younger boys while he began his work.

"Chad walked his brothers over to the local mercantile. He had no money to buy anything, not even a piece of one-cent candy, but being in the big city was exciting, and he just wanted to look around. Entering the store was like eye-candy for the boys. They quietly walked around each aisle and peered into each counter of treasures, being careful not to touch anything. Chad noticed a poster on the wall. He didn't read well, but on the sign he saw the image of a piece of art. Going to the counter where the store-merchant stood, he asked about the poster.

"*'Oh, that. Yep, its an art contest'* explained the store clerk.

"*'What's the prize?'* asked Chad.

"*'Hmmm, let me see'* The storekeeper peered closer at the poster. *'Says it's two-fifty for the winner.'.* Chad thought about all the candy he buy for himself and the others for two dollars!

"*'When is the contest?'* Chad asked.

"*'Boy, you're pesky. Ok, says it's today, and the judgin' at 3 p.m. at the hotel.'*

"'Chad's spirits bottomed. *Today*, he thought, *Oh, but I still have time! It's only mid-morning.* Chad took his brothers out of the store and stood for at least five minutes on the boardwalk thinking. His eyes grew big and bright. *'I've got it!'* He guided his obedient brothers to the back alley, in hopes of finding supplies to create a winning project."

Grandma paused and looked around the table to make sure we were on the edge of our seat before she continued.

"Coming out of the alley, he carried scraps of burlap, a discarded poster-board with the words *lait maternel* on it, and some moldy fruit he'd use for coloring. He didn't know what the poster-board words said, but it was colorful against the burlap, so he decided to use the word-side of the board. Sitting himself down on the far end of the boardwalk, away from the stores and crowds, he removed his pocket knife and began his art project.

"Periodically, he walked the brothers around so that they wouldn't complain too much. After four hours of creating, Chad finished. *'Come on. We don't have much time'*. He took the art to the hotel and asked where he could sign up for the contest. '*I'm sorry, son. The contest is closed. The judges will start any minute now.*'

"Chadwallder was not to be dismissed", Grandma Jane said in an Irish accent. "In pure Irish gusto, he begged the lady to allow him to put his art with the others. She looked down at Chad, and the other boys, and agreed. '*You look like such sweet children. Ok, let's see what we can do*'.

"The nice hotel-lady placed Chad's burlap artwork next to a beautifully crafted painting with several similar art works placed around the room. These paintings were made from the best store-bought materials. Chad understood that his artwork did not compare in quality, but this didn't dissuade him. His work was different, but it was good," Grandma admonished.

"'*What's your name*', she asked, '*so I can write it on the place-card in front of your art.*'

"'*My name is Chadwallder Ambrose Blayney* , was his answer, and so she wrote: Chadwallder A. Blaney. Chad didn't know any different, so he didn't correct the spelling of his last name.

"'*When will the judging begin?*' Chad asked. '*Well, it's 3 o'clock now, so I guess any minute. We need to leave the room and wait in the lobby. The judges will tell the assembly of their decision.*'

"Chad, Loulis, and Cian waited in the lobby of this fancy hotel, for what seemed like hours. There were finely dressed men with finely dressed women, by their sides. Chad and the boys wore pants too short for their growing bodies, shoes with gaping holes and patchwork on their jackets. They each wore newspaper-boy wool caps but had removed them entering the hotel. It was evident to Chad that he was different. His younger siblings were oblivious to the social-economic differences, which Chad thought was a blessing.

"Finally," Grandma said softly, "the judges emerged from the side parlor where all the wonderful artwork was displayed. The judges were as equally well dressed and distinguished - looking as those anxiously waiting to hear the judging results. Clearing his throat, the judge, that appeared to be in charge, began.

"'This year's charity art contest has produced outstanding quality and beauty. The proceeds of the sales, from these paintings, will no doubt bring a wealth of funds to our orphanage. We would like to thank each of you for your submissions, dedication to our cause and your talent. However, we have an unusual yet stunning entry. So, in keeping with the spirit of helping our city's less fortunate children, we award first prize to the artwork of Chadwallder A. Blaney.'

"Chad was stunned!" Grandma said exaggerating *stunned*. "He had been stoically hopeful, but underneath, he didn't think he stood a chance. Now, it was real. He had won.

"His artwork of a 3- foot, free-standing, burlap, silhouetted self-image had won. He didn't know, when he was working on the piece, that the contest was for an orphanage and that the image of an orphaned-looking boy against the poster of **Mother's Milk** would be significant. He had created it from his talent, his heart and the supplies he found in the garbage alley.

"'Could Mr. Blaney please step forward for our congratulations and acknowledgment,' announced the second judge.

"'Shyly, Chad stepped from the crowded room and toward the judges. Their faces were both in awe and surprise. '*Son',* the third judge spoke as he held up the burlap art. *'Is this your art?.'*

"'*Yes, sir, 'tis*', Chad said humbly. A round of loud applause broke out. When it had died down, Chad looked up from his shoes and noticed many of the fancy-dressed women had tears in their eyes.

"'*Well, son. Here is your price. Twenty-five dollars'.*

"'*How much*?' Chad asked in disbelief.

"'*Here's a check for $25.00. First price!'* Grandma said in pride as if she had won the prize."

Grandma Jane continued to tell details of the events that followed after Chad had accepted the check. Twenty-five dollars in the late 1800s was equivalent to three-hundred today, Grandma boasted! They purchased food and shoes for all the children and a new kettle for Oliver's new bride.

My mind went to brother Nathanial and the similarities of the two boy's natural artistic talent, yet, to date, I had never even heard the name Chadwallder.

What I had managed to put on a shelf, was now back in my lap. On top of recounting the near-drowning episode, I was confronted with two other pieces of information: The first was the similarities between Nathanial and this boy named, Chad. I had said that very name out loud during the picnic in the Redwoods. How would I have known that name? Secondly, I wondered what

Grandma meant about Oliver's *new bride*. Was that who Fanny was speaking to? *Ma, help me*.

Before leaving that Sunday, I found Grandma Jane in the kitchen alone. "Grandma, you said Oliver had a new wife. What did you mean?"

"Well, Amelia, times were hard back then, and sometimes women died in childbirth or shortly after that. Fanny's mother, Lucinda, my grandmother, died when Fanny was young. Oliver remarried shortly after that".

"How young was Fanny when her mom died? I questioned.

"I think 10 or 11," was her answer, but then she immediately went on. "But, Amelia, that doesn't mean your mom will die. It was just the hard times of a century ago."

"I know,"I reassured her. The truth was that I was not thinking about losing my mom. I was thinking about Fanny's cry for help when she was perhaps my age and drowning. It's possible that her mom was already dead at that time.

Goose-bumps ran down my arms as I turned on my heels and left Grandma drying dishes.

Fanny was talking to her dead mother.

4

Sunflowers

I didn't know where the time went. I just remembered being 12 one day, and then my childhood was gone.

From 1967, and our magical California vacation, until 1972, time was a blur and seemed more like a framed family photo than a real experience.

My carefree life of reading mysteries and hiding out above the garage, was replaced with teenage social life and making good grades, in preparation for college. My personality was quiet and unquestioning in those years. I respected my parents, and if they said college was the right future then college was my only path. I would be allowed to select my career or academic road, but only with their approval.

With this intent in mind, I took advanced math and science classes and spent a great deal of my alone-time hitting the books. I was an A student. The exception was in courses such as Home Economics. I had little interest in baking principles or how to sew an apron. In this apathetic mode, I mindlessly threw my used chewing-gum in the flour bin during a cooking class and as I glanced up, I saw the teacher wide-eyed and frozen in disbelief. I was not a wife-hopeful or the teacher's favorite. I squeaked by with a C.

College-prep was not the only stressor. Teenage peer pressure was enormous; *wear the right clothes* and *have the right hair*. The on-slot of hormones scored equally as stressful. I saw my body changing, starting with my menstrual cycle at age 13, and in perfect unison with my unusual moodiness. This behavior change even puzzled me, at times. It was the perfect storm, at age 17, for what was about to happen next.

Perry was handsome but not very popular. That was not important to me. What attracted me was something different. He was smart and old for his 17 years. We could talk all afternoon about serious things and nothing really at all. I had grown into a reasonably attractive girl with long dark wavy hair. My hazel eyes were still large but had grown into my face. I often wore my hair up on my head, and Perry liked it that way. He said my neck was elegant, and that made me smile.

We were good friends — until we were more. I cannot remember how it happened, exactly, except that we were at his house and thoroughly enjoying each other's company in the basement family room. His parents were gardening out back. We'd been in a deep conversation about how our high school years were playing out and how we couldn't wait to be adults and living on our own. We mused about sharing an apartment downtown, eating out every meal, and going to bed whenever we wanted to. We would laugh at each junction, pause and start up again with another adult-life fantasy.

Then, it just happened. Perry leaned forward and kissed me. We had never kissed before. We had held hands once, while walking in the park, but we both seemed taken back by the act and released hands as quickly as we'd begun.

His kiss was warm, and I melted into his embrace. Later, I would wonder how much of what happened was the result of raging hormones or because I wasn't brave enough to stop — afraid he wouldn't like me as much if I did.

When we came up for air, the embarrassment of my pants off and underwear at my ankles, was unbearable. I quickly gathered my clothes and fastened my hair back in a bun. I could barely look at Perry, who was breathlessly now lying on his back. I sat up, looking just at my feet before saying,   "What just happened? Perry, we shouldn't have done that!".

"I know," he said, still catching his breath, "but we did."

Feeling like a different creature, I could do nothing but leave as quickly as possible. Certain that the word *sex* was written all over my face, I crept into my house and bedroom without anyone noticing. Relieved to be safely in my space, I quietly wept.

That day changed our relationship, and for three months we barely spoke. I had felt sick about what had happened, but mostly, I felt sick about the loss of his friendship. I was in turmoil, and the one person I could have gone to was the one person I couldn't approach now — or at least until it was necessary to do so. With every ounce of courage that I could drum up, I called his house.

"Hello, Mrs. Driscoll, this is Amelia. Is Perry in?"

"Of course, Amelia. We've missed you around here, Everything ok with you and your family?" she replied.

"Oh yes, just fine, thank you."

"Ok, I'll get Perry. Hold on".

It seemed like an hour went by before he came on the line. "Hello," he greeted.

"Hi, it's me," I said timidly.

"Amelia, hi" How are you?"

"Fine," I said, and then there was a long pause. "No, I guess I'm not fine, Perry. Can we meet?

"Sure. Now?" he asked.

"Yes, if that's ok."

"Meet me at Mason's in 15". Mason's was a small city park located between our two homes. We would often make this our meet-up place before going into town or deciding what we were going to do that day.

Hanging up the phone, I ran to the bathroom with bile in my throat. My stomach had not been right for some time, and now it felt like gravel was rumbling around in there. It caught in my throat and I released my breakfast in the toilet.

Where did that carefree girl go — the one that loved to watch how birds methodically gathered dried twigs to build a nest? I said quietly to myself.

She's in the dark, icy waters, was the reply.

Perry was right on-time. Our eyes met, and the pain of that changed relationship was evident on both of our faces. "Hi," he said.

"Hi," I returned.

We found a park bench and sat. No one else was around, and for that I was grateful. Over the next 10 minutes, I told Perry about my persistent nausea, reading the school nurse materials on pregnancy and about visiting the county public health care clinic, testing positive that I was pregnant. I paused with this chronological story-telling and waited.

Perry was quiet then, "but we only did it once!" was his disappointing response.

"Yep, and now there's one baby," I quipped in irritation. We sat a little longer without talking. Sensing there was nothing more to say, I stood and faced him. His eyes slowly wandered up to meet mine.

"What will you do?" he asked.

"I don't know."

"Have you told your parents?"

"No, I wanted to tell you first. I'm going to tell them tonight."

"Oh," was his only and final response. At that, I turned and walked back home.

I did tell my parents but not for another three days. I don' know what a 17-year-old expects when she tells her baby's father she is pregnant, but Perry's reaction had left me empty. It took those three days to refill my brave-meter.

My parents were stunned, angry and disappointed, but within the hour they generously offered their love and support. I'm sure my news was painful for them, primarily since my dad was a preacher but throughout the pregnancy, all they showed me was love. I didn't feel I deserved it, but they gave it anyway. In those days, girls that got pregnant at 17, dropped out of school or were sent away to have the baby. My parents wouldn't hear of either. My dad arranged, with the high school, for me to continue my education at the local technical college. The plan was for me to have this baby and my high school diploma, *so you have choices, Amelia*, was Mom's sage advice.

While my father didn't ask me, I choose to stop attending church services. The decision was more than the obvious. The truth was I had stopped believing in the organizational religious aspects of faith and didn't want to be there, especially under the anticipated glaring eyes as my belly grew.

In my eighth month, Mom announced, "this is a great time to pull out my ancestry research. I was pregnant with Sam when I started it. Let's do that now, Amelia." I had lost my desire to know about Frances and Chad. Those days and memories had faded through the years. But I didn't want to disappoint Mom. "Sure. Let's do that," I said with a half-smile.

We began by looking at her tattered, yellowed, handwritten notes, accompanied by old newspaper clippings and Xeroxed copies of pages. One of the first things that caught my eye was this notation: *It seems that Grandma Frances was nicked name, Fanny.*

Fanny. But the note went on. *Fanny, my grandmother, was the youngest of 12 children. Six of the children were full siblings. Then her mother, Lucinda Jane, died at age 40. Fanny was eleven at the time of her mother's death. Oliver, my great-grandfather, remarried within a year to Jane Reid who had three children of her own . Oliver and Jane had three more. Fanny was the oldest girl.*

Fanny was eleven when her mother died and her dad remarried by the time she was twelve When I was 12, I was…

Then it hit me. When I was 12, I was drowning. I was drowning and Fanny was talking.

"Fanny, are you sure? The water is now warm, and the sun is bright with hope. Are you sure?" Was she talking to her dead mother or herself? I still didn't know for sure but wondered if the death of her mother, when Fanny was 11, had something to do with all of this.

These words, reverberated in my head, were as if I were back in the waters. Did Fanny try to kill herself? Where was she that I heard this so clearly? Thoughts were swirling all around me as I turned to my mom and asked, "Mom, in your research, did you find anything about Fanny nearly drowning?"

"No, Amelia, nothing like that, although I saw an article. Let's see. It is here someplace... Oh, here it is; a picture of a small lake with a wooden dock that I think was on their property. When my great-grandfather emigrated from Ireland, the land was granted to his family for some service he had performed for King George. It was evidently a big scandal among the Irish kindship that he served for the King of England."

She paused, and I was silent for a moment.

"Amelia, does this have anything to do with the time you were lost in the ocean? I remember you asking a lot of questions about this back then".

"I don't know," I replied. "I think maybe... it's not impossible, right? My great-grandmother couldn't possibly be a part of that, right?"

Mom looked at me, and I saw a peculiar look on her face as if to say, *there's something I need to tell you.* Instead, we grew

silent again and continued to sort through the research material
aimlessly.

She pulled out a boot box and opened the lid. This box
resembled a shoebox only it had held a newly bought pair of work
boots for dad when he was a younger man. Inside the box were a
pile of black and white photos. Mom scooped up the collection
and laid them on the kitchen table. The first picture she pulled out
was of a young girl. Her hair was long and pulled back, but it was
full and wavy like mine. She wasn't smiling, and her eyes were
forlorn. Looking closer, I saw that she wore a dress that went to
her ankles.

My face turned pale, and I sat paralyzed — my eyes wide
open. The dress was dark, maybe brown, with a print of large
sunflowers.

"Mom!" I shouted. "Who is this?"

"Well, that's Fanny, Amelia, your great-grandmother. She
looks a little like you, don't you think?"

5

Cross Overs

That day, looking at the old photographs, my life shifted in
ways I couldn't have fully understood at the time. What I did
know, was that it was time to talk with my grandma. All the

coincidences around Fanny and my near drowning had to mean something. Grandma would have some answers for me.

A few days later, I invited myself over for tea. The bonus was Grandma's famous gingerbread cake, topped with homemade applesauce, served with a dollop of whipping cream. I didn't come for the cake, but it didn't hurt, either.

Her home was warm, as she always had a little wood-burning stove glowing heat. It was a narrow, black, free-standing chimney that stood in the kitchen and served as an extra stove top. On the stove, Grandma kept a pot of boiling water so that tea was *at the ready* for invited and uninvited guests. She was a part of a large community of American-Irish women, who lived in the same neighborhood. I never tired of watching the ritual as Grandma and another Irish woman greeted each other. The custom, born of poverty and probably a left over from the Irish potato famine, was to ask *and* refuse twice before accepting any food. It went like this:

"Oh how lovely to see you, Mary. Would you like a cup of tea and a piece of cake?" Grandma Jane would say.

"Jane, you are so kind. Tea would be lovely but no cake. I'm watching my waistline," her guest would reply. Tea would be served in short order with the following offer (number two).

"Are you sure you don't want any cake?"

"Oh no, love, the tea is all I need." With that, they would chat for a few more minutes. If Grandma didn't have any cake, there would be no more offer of dessert, and she would have kept her good host reputation. The third offer, of the cake, was the magic. If an Irish woman offers food the third time, that means she it to offer, and the guest can accept.

"Mary, it's a lovely gingerbread cake. Couldn't I serve you a small piece? You can watch that waistline tomorrow."

"Oh, dear, you are so persuasive. I'll take a small sliver, then."

It was apparent, to me, that Grandma Jane had cake. The house was permeated with the sweet smell of ginger and apples. She only asked once, and I accepted. I knew the ritual, but I was too eager for the cake to play it out.

We sat down, in her cozy kitchen, sipping tea and eating cake. We were silent, at first, but we both knew this visit had a purpose. "*A leanbh*, your mother tells me that you have some questions for me about your great-grandmother?" I remained silent, as I internally smiled at the familiar term of affection: *A leanbh*, meaning "my child," as well as the need to gather my thought on how to best approach the topic.

"Yes, Grandma. Do you remember when I nearly drowned in the California Ocean?" I asked.

"Of course, Amelia. That was very scary for us all, and I imagine especially for you."

"Well, I have a story to tell you and then my questions," I interjected. She waited patiently, and I began. I told her about the voice I had heard while in the water, the names Mary Ann and hearing my own name, about the picture of Fanny in the dress, her eyes and her hair and the similarities with Nathanial and Chad. When done, I realized I had been talking fast and breathless as I finally said, "Grandma, I think your mother came to me in the water! How can that be?"

Grandma Jane sat poised. Her face glowed rosy cheeks that were kind and gentle. She was in her 80's, without any wrinkles, and her thick white hair was long but always up in a French twist secured with sizable wooden hair pens. I looked at her, and her serene face was caring as she reached over and took my hand off the fork, I had been tightly holding during my story.

"Amelia, I believe you did have an experience with my mother. I think your near-drowning experience crossed over to her near drowning when she was 12. Now, I'm going to tell you a story, and I want you to listen carefully. Are you ready?"

"Yes," was all I could muster.

"My mother, your great-grandmother, had a rough life. She didn't talk about it often but in very much the same way that we need to talk about this now, she talked with me about my experience. I, too, had a cross-over when I was 15. I met my grandfather, Oliver, down by the Satsop River."

I knew the Satsop River. On our biannual trips to the ocean, we would pass by Grandma's childhood town of Montesano. The river looped through town, crossing under the main highway toward the coast. "I went to the river to think," Grandma began. "I did that often and usually brought my journal with me to write down my thoughts. This time, however, I aimlessly walked and found myself at the river's edge.

"My father had denied me the chance to go with some friends into Olympia to a dance, and I was very sad and a bit angry at him. I sat on a rock near the river and cried. To conceal my tears, should anyone happen by, I took my hair out of my bonnet. My hair back then was thick and wavy like yours is now. I rarely had it down because it was unmanageable and would get too tangled if left to dangle in the wind but also because, back then, a lady wore a hat when in public. That was just how it was." I nodded in complete understanding. My hair was a wild mess if I didn't hold it back in a ponytail or up on my head. It was the family curse of hair!

Knowing I understood, Grandma squeezed my hand lightly and continued. "Amelia, what I'm going to tell you may be a bit scary, but I think it's time you know." At this, my stomach churned ,but I trusted that if my Grandma was telling me something, it was important, and it was true. I nodded that I was ready.

"My mother, your great grandmother, had the same dark and wavy hair that you have. When I took my hair down and was feeling all this sorrow for missing out on a trip with my friends, the air around me swirled, and the atmosphere changed. Looking up through the veil of my hair, I saw him.

"He stood on the river's edge, feet halfway in the water. He wore a pair of worn overalls, clearly hand-made, and brogans on his feet. He wore a cap on his head that appeared to be wool because I could see moth-holes in the sides. He tipped his hat to me and said, *'Mornin' ma'am. Surely sorry for your loss. My name is Oliver Blayney'.*

" I was frightened at first but somehow knew that he was both not real and not talking to me. He seemed to be looking right past me, and he was not aware that his boots were in the water.

Still startled, I stood up quickly, pulled my hair back up and out of my eyes, and when I did that, he disappeared".

"What was it?" I asked.

"It was my mother's father, my grandfather who emigrated from Ireland to Canada midcentury. I ran home and told my mother what had happened. That is when she told me her story and the story her mother had told her. Amelia, it's hard to understand, but it's about our hair. When your hair is down, and you are feeling something intense, you have a portal into another time and place."

"I don't understand. When I went into the ocean, I had my hair up tight on my head and in a cap, so that can't be it," I argued.

"But was your hair still in the cap when you were sinking?" she asked. I remembered, then, that the bathing cap had come off in the heavy waves, during our body surfing, and my hair had released. "Amelia, there's nothing for you to fear. You can control this, and so can your mother, and so can I. What happened to you was that during a time that you were scared of the water's control over your body, you joined with your great grandmother's similar experience."

"Then she nearly drowned, too?" I asked.

Grandma Jane told me the story of how Lucinda Jane Blayney, Fanny's mother, died when Fanny was only eleven, and as the oldest girl, she became the mother, housekeeper, and woman-of-the-house. She had been very close to her mother, and her death had devastated Fanny emotionally. Just a year after her mother's death, Oliver met and married a local woman whose husband had also died the same year as Lucinda.

Together, the family grew to 9 children and Fanny would be expected to do much of the chores and care of the children. At the news that her father was marrying Jane Reid, with her three children in tow, Fanny was emotionally drained. She walked to the lake on their property with the intent of ending her life. Grandma Jane said that she didn't know if Fanny had actually jumped in because the story was never told past the point of Fanny standing on the small wooden dock.

"I still don't get it. What is it we are experiencing?" I asked, not considering there would be a clearer explanation.

"Here's what I think, *A leanbh*. I think time and space overlap. We can't comprehend this because all we see is our present time. But other times are replaying or maybe actually happening simultaneously. I don't know. When I look at my experience and the stories my mother told me about hers and now your story, it appears there's no actual interaction between the two but we merely see our ancestors in their time while we are here in ours."

"But, she called my name!" I rebutted.

"Maybe, but perhaps she was referring to her sisters; Amelia and Mary Ann. She was rethinking her decision to end her life in consideration of what it would do to her sisters left behind. What is curious is that she couldn't have been talking out loud, in the water, so you heard her thoughts."

Being pregnant threw all rational emotional responses sideways. So, on top of that and this information from my grandma, it all seemed too much to process. I began to weep. Grandma was quietly crying, as well. She reached over, in what I thought would be a touch of my hand to comfort me. Instead, she took down my hair and then took down her hair, too.

Grandma and I didn't talk about what happened next, until a few weeks later. It was enough to have experienced the family gift together without examining it thoroughly. I tended to think about things in a logical way, but there would be no reasonable explanation to what had happened.

Three weeks after that time in her kitchen, I went into labor. I had just turned 18 the week before, May 16th. Perry and I had only spoke twice during the pregnancy. We had made no plans to see each other or to raise this child jointly. Without extended conversations, with my parents, it was understood that I was going to keep this baby. My father had been under enormous pressure, from the elders of the church, to sweep my sins away. The encouraged him to *place* the baby under adoption and pretend the pregnancy never happened. But he held firm in support of his family and love for me. It angered me that they would be so judgmental and pushy about something that was none of their business, and I would think on that well into my future career. I also felt shame and guilt to be the cause of Dad's suffering.

Two years after the baby's birth, Dad voluntarily left the formal ministry to co-found a mission for unwed mothers. It seemed the consequences of my in-the-moment passion changed more than two lives forever.

The labor was drama, drama, and more drama. I was young and had never experienced pain like that before. I had taken prenatal-classes, with Mom as my coach and seen all the real life videos and explanations of what childbirth would be like, but none of it prepared me for a basketball exiting my privates. I cried and screamed without reserve with each contraction. I yelled, "Make it stop!" many times and, "I've changed my mind!" a few others.

When the contractions were two minutes apart, something came over me. It was a calmness and an internal voice leading me forward. I took my hair band out and purposed my long, unmanageable hair to fall across my shoulders. My Mom gasped. "Are you sure, Amelia?"

"No, but I think I need this," was my quiet response.

All the planning for this baby's birth came together in my third trimester — the crib, the stroller, the blankets and diapers set up in the corner of my room and the picking of names: if it's a girl she'll be called Fionna Jane; if a boy, Liam Keagan. Although somewhat detached from this planning, I was fully present now and wanted this experience to be rich and memorable. Grandma Jane said I could control this family gift, and this seemed an excellent time to test out that theory.

The contractions moved closer and closer together and then I was taken into the delivery room. Two weeks earlier, we had given the birthing center a music cassette to play during delivery. When I was wheeled into the harshly lite delivery room, a Celtic tune was playing. Dr. Kiefer dimmed the lights, against hospital policy, and playfully said, "Now young lady, let's have a baby."

What happened next would be replayed in my mind for years to come. The cross-over would be a mixture of my present and Fanny's past. I saw, simultaneously, my delivery room and also a small dark room that appeared to be in a house.

My room was filled with the modern medical equipment, and my legs and feet were in obstetric- stirrups. As I flashed to the other scene, my legs were merely bent at the knees while I lay on a mattress near the floor.

Dr. Kiefer gave me instructions when to push. At the same time, an old women, dressed in a nearly-white apron, spoke similar instructions to her patient.

Dr. Kiefer wore scrubs and a surgical cap while the old woman wore a maid's cotton bonnet. Back and forth, I attended both births…I *was* both births… alternating between the present time of 1973 and a small private room, at the turn of the century.

I was not frightened or alarmed. I heard my moans and grunts with each push and I heard hers as well.

'Push, hard now, ma'am", the old women said.

"I can't do anymore!", the unseen woman anguished.

"Ms. O'Malley, you must push!" repeated the old women in a thick Irish accent.

As if in a dream, I thought for just for a moment, that her hand was reaching through time to hold my hand, giving us both the strength for the final push. Only then did I understand that I was witnessing Fanny's labor while I was experiencing the pains of my own.

The final push was the delivery for us both.

"It's a boy," proclaimed Dr. Kiefer.

"It's a wee baby boy," announced the old woman.

"His name will be Byron," Fanny said through her exhaustion.

6

All Formless

The day after Byron's birth, I told Mom the story of birthing with Fanny and she smiled pleasingly, but we rarely spoke of it again.

They say you forget the horrible birthing pain once your baby is in your arms. I think that is because you are too tired to even remember your name. This was my reality, and for the next several months our home was filled with sleepless nights, diapers to wash and naps to take whenever possible. The decision to name *my* baby boy, Byron, was spontaneous but with certainty. Lord Byron was one of my favorite poets, and his words kept rising in my ear;

Deep sleep came down on every eye save mine—

And there it stood,—all formless—but divine

Byron James O'Malley Nolan. The middle name was after my father who gave up his quiet life as a minister, to love his daughter instead. I didn't know if Fanny chose the name Byron for the same love of this poet or if hearing the name prompted my recall. Either way, *Byron* was perfect for us both.

My brothers had long since flown the coup. James Jr. was off and married to Jasmin and started a family of their own. The twins finished college and both worked as engineers at a local airplane manufacturing plant; Stephen was engaged to be married, and Paddy already married to Twila. Jack was in med- school, starting his residency soon in Nebraska and Samuel was still deciding what he wanted to do with his life as he entered into his second year of college.

Nathanial was traveling up and down the Pacific coast mostly staying in the San Francisco Bay area, creating art and immersing himself in that community. He said that college was not right for him but he would learn more from real-life.

Byron and I remained living with Mom and Dad. When he was nearly 2 1/2 years old, I decided it was time to get a job and begin my own life. My parents periodically mention the hope for college, but I couldn't imagine college as a part of my future now. Instead, over the past two years, I had devoured any book I could find having to do with psychology or how the mind worked.

Interestingly enough, I wasn't drawn to the paranormal field but had a keen interest in understanding how we came to conclusions or how we processed thought. While my brain was fuzzy so much of the time, due to sleep deprivation, I determined myself to use Byron's nap-time to read and absorb.

I had grown dependent on my family to watch over and provide for us. I had little confidence that I could take care of myself, let alone a baby. The brave and feisty little 12-year old was gone, and what remained was a 20-year-old relying on others for the basics of food and shelter. I knew it was time to gain my own independence, even if in short measure.

In baby steps toward adulthood, I got a secretary's job in August of 1975, at the local University's Admission Office. I figured that if I couldn't go to college, at least I could be in that environment. Mom agreed to care for Byron while I was at work, Monday through Thursday. I loved the University atmosphere. People, not so different from my age, were walking around, learning, and improving their lives. I understood that the cute little gal flirting with the handsome jock did not have a 2-year-old at home, but I was still sure we wanted the same chance at happiness.

During lunch breaks, I would take my sack lunch and walk over to a shaded court-yard, not too far from the office. I would sit there, just watching and listening. On Tuesday, my third week of employment, a tall and handsome guy walked in front of me, and I gasped. He heard the primal noise and turned to look at me. It was Perry.

It had been three years since I had last seen him. He had grown from a high school adolescent to a handsome young man and seeing him took my breath away…hence…the gasp.

"Amelia!" he said with excitement. He sat down next to me, and we began to talk. It was the same easy talking that we'd exchanged a few years ago. Our connection had not been lost .

We met the next day again, at the same spot. He asked if I would walk with him to his next class. As we walked, there was a silence. Then he asked about the baby.

I told him about Byron and a little about the birth (minus the part about being in two birthing rooms at the same time). I told him about Byron's dark curly hair, blue eyes and dimpled chin. Perry's eyes were blue, while mine were hazel. Perry listened with interest.

"Amelia, I know I wasn't there for you during the pregnancy, and you'd have every right to say no, but could I meet him? We don't have to tell him I'm his father." I didn't have to think about it and I wasn't upset with Perry for being absent during my pregnancy.

"Yes!" I said. "Would you like to come over tonight for dinner?"

I presented the invitation before asking Mom, but it felt right. My parents had wanted me to contact Perry throughout the pregnancy and make him take responsibility for my *condition,* but I had refused. Now, I was not sure how they would react to his sudden presence in our home.

Perry did come to dinner that night and was there many nights from then on. My parents were cautious and protective, but gracious to Perry within a short time. Perry and Byron played on the floor and there was considerable pleasure between the two of them. When Byron would go to bed, Perry and I would retreat to the back porch where we would sit and talk. In anticipation, and no surprise, we kissed the third night together. "Amelia, I want us to date and see how this goes."

Date?

I had never thought of dating while I had a baby, but I was touched that Perry wanted to date me ,not just assume a role of being here at the house. "Wow. Yes, I think that's great!"

And so the courtship began and continued into the New Year. It was a hybrid of dating with the restriction of being a mother to a toddler. Some of our dates included Byron, and most of them were low-budget because neither of us had vast financial resources.

Perry had a studio-apartment but we agreed that, for now ,we wouldn't go there and be alone. Instead, there were picnics at the park, trips to the petting zoo, burgers at the new McDonalds in town and, my favorite, going to the library. We always stop at a Dairy Queen for a chocolate dipped cone after the library dates.

"Amelia," he began as we exited the library eight months into our dating, "Why aren't you in college? You're smart and need to be going for a degree!"

I was taken back by his question and observation. I had not even considered that I could go to college, have a job and raise a child. I assumed that my life was directed differently now.

"Well, for one, I can't afford college, and two, I have to work, and three, Perry, I'm a single Mom," was my sassy reply.

"I have an idea but give me a few days before I tell you," Perry said. "In the meantime, let's go have a Dilly Bar *and* an ice cream cone!" We laughed, and the affection between us was tangible.

Three days passed and it was now mid-week, late afternoon in April. I got off of work at 4 and Perry was waiting for me at the bus station. Perry was there with his 1967 Ford Comet to pick me up, and give me a lift home.

I was surprised to see him since we had not made plans to meet. We had a date-night planned for the weekend; going to a local coffee shop near Point Defiance to hear a local band. Seeing him was a delight and surprise.

"Hi. What are you doing here?" I asked with a big smile.

"I told you I had an idea and I couldn't wait to tell you!" Perry blurted out.

Perry drove us down to Steilacoom Lake. We parked the car and he got out. I paused long enough that he was able to rush over to my door and open it for me. *Charming*, I thought. We walked to the water's edge and sat on a bench overlooking the lake. In the winter, this part of the lake would freeze over, and patrons could skate on it. Today it was 63 degrees and mild...no ice skating today.

"OK," he said with excitement. "I've done my research and here's a plan."

" Marry me," he abruptly said. "No wait, there's more. We would qualify for married student housing, an apartment right on campus, and Byron could go to the daycare program there, too. You could easily get a Pell Grant for your education, and we'd both be students at the University." He continued; "I've spoken with your Dad, and he has given his blessing."

I was stunned. It was not at all what I had expected, but I was not put off either. I loved Perry, and I was clear about that. He had already told me he loved me, too. He had taken the time and energy to research this thoroughly, and I felt that love. I smiled and remained silent. With that, he bent on one knee, presented a small diamond ring and did it properly.

"Amelia Jane O'Malley Nolan, will you marry me and put me out of my misery of living a life without you?"

I wanted this moment to last forever, and without reasonable thought, I removed the two bobby pins holding up my hair, letting it cascade down over my shoulders and said emphatically- "Yes!"

What happened next made that moment all the more magical. Surrounding Perry and I, only visible to me, were children dancing. It was the same vision Grandma Jane and I experienced that day in her kitchen. There were at least a dozen children in a circle moving in hops and jumps. There was a fiddle playing Celtic music in the background, and the children smiled and jumped higher each time the lively chorus came in. My spirit was soaring as if I were dancing too. I started tapping my foot to the music that wasn't really there. Perry laughed at my gaiety without understanding its source.

That day, with the magical proposal and the family gift at play, I was certain would remain as a sacred memory forever.

––––––––––––

Two weeks after our cross over together, Grandma Jane and I looked at the photos tucked away in Mom's boot box. Grandma Jane had a few of her own to bring out onto her long dining room table. In our memories of the dancing children, we both saw each child's face, their smiles, hair, eyes and even a few that laughed out loud. One by one, except for two children present, we were able to match a child's face with a family photo. Without exception, we both selected the same pictures of the children we saw in the crossover. From Mom's research, we had names and birth dates to attach to these photos.

Fanny, probably around 12 at the time of party, was holding the hand of what appeared to be the youngest sibling named Cian, age two, and on the other side of Cian was two older siblings, Sarah and Jeanette. These were Fanny's stepsisters from the union of Oliver and Jane Reid. On the right side of Sarah the sizes of children cascaded from smaller to larger; Mary Ann, Amelia, Loulis and Samuel.

Clapping happily, but not in the circle, was Chadwallder, the favorite brother who was closest in age to Fanny. There were two other children we couldn't identify from our photos. It was not likely they were from the Blayney-clan, as all nine children were present.

Was this the wedding celebration for Oliver and Jane? We didn't see any adults, not even the fiddler, in our cross-over visitation. It was as before. We were present in their time without them interacting with us.

I didn't consciously chose the same vision during Perry's proposal that I had experienced with Granda Jane but I *wanted* that pure joy again of children dancing. I wondered if I had controlled the coming of this particular vision. It appeared I could choose, or at least I did this time.

———————————

Neither Perry nor I wanted a big wedding. But Mom had a different wish. I was her only daughter and that tradition, according to Mom, was that a daughter's parents throw the big celebration while a son's parents participate minimally. Mom was not pushy but requested there be lots of flowers, at least two bridesmaids and groomsman, a flower girl, ring bearer, white linen, and music.

The compromise was satisfactory. We planned a backyard wedding with the altar area overlooking the back orchard. Mom stayed busy showing me pictures of flowers and rented chairs eager to have me make a decision. It wasn't hard to do. Her love and patience with me, during my pregnancy, was a tremendous gift to me. I could give her this and enjoy it, too. Perry was easy going, and while he had an opinion on *this* over *that,* he just rolled with the punches.

We selected magnolias as our theme-flower and Mom did the rest. Next was creating the guest list. Brothers James, Stephen, Patrick, and Samuel were easy to recruit for help. Jack would fly in a few days before the wedding. Perry asked my five brothers to be groomsman, along with his friend, Troy, as his best man. This left me to come up with five bridesmaids. I had been very private during the past three years because of my pregnancy, but I had befriended a few ladies in my office. There was also Jasmin and Twila, my brothers' wives, to think about as choices. I liked all of them very much.

Finding Nathanial however, was proving to be difficult. I wanted Nathanial to be my best person. I knew it was unorthodox to have a male in this honored position but it's want I wanted. Nathanial and I had been in touch periodically the past year. I knew, now, why he was missing-in-action. Last April, he called me and told me he was gay. He was afraid the family wouldn't understand and couldn't bear to have Dad's disapproval. For that reason, he wasn't going to come home anytime soon. It had been two months since I had been able to reach him and now that phone number had been disconnected. I wrote him three letters in June to the only known address in San Francisco. Two letters were returned, *address unknown*. As my wedding day approached, August 14th, 1976, I was sad about Nathanial not being there.

Finally, late in July, he called. "Nathanial!" Mom proclaimed as she picked up the phone. "Are you ok? Where are you?" she fussed. I sat nearby holding my breath hoping he wasn't calling from a hospital or jail, and that he was well and happy. They exchanged a few more words but Mom quickly handed me the phone. "He'll only talk with you," she said irritated.

"Nathanial, I've been trying to reach you. Where are you?"

"I'm at the gas station on the corner. I want to come home, but I'm scared. I got your letter that you're getting married. I couldn't miss that and I want to meet my nephew....but I'm scared." I could tell he was crying.

"I'll be right there. Don't move". At that, I quickly hung up and told Mom I would be right back. I ran the quarter of a mile to the Shell station. There was Nathanial, sitting on the two-foot concrete wall barrier. He saw me, jumped up and ran to meet me. We embraced in a tight hold and Nathanial wept. He was rail-thin.

"I don't know what will happen or even if you need to disclose anything right now. But Nathanial, I do know that your family loves you. And I know that you need some fattening up". We both laughed a nervously and slowly walked back home.

In the front yard stood Dad anxiously waiting. We'd been walking arm in arm approaching the house but when Nathanial saw Dad, his arms fell away and his pace slowed. I walked into the house leaving them there alone.

Watching from the living room window, I saw them embrace and hold that hug for a few minutes while Dad talked in Nathanial's ear. When they came into the house they were both quiet. Mom grabbed Nathanial for her turn in the hugging. "Let's get you something to eat. Dinner won't be ready for a few hours," she said as she released him than she walked into the kitchen to begin her magic. Nathanial turned to me and smiled slightly. "I didn't tell him, but I think he might know," he said as he walked by me following Mom.

Mom made an extra special dinner resembling Thanksgiving the next night. She said Nathanial's return was a reason to give thanks and a good excuse to gather the clan for a family reunion. The dinner was full of laughter, food, and family. We were all there, with spouses, fiancés, and girlfriends. Byron was not the youngest, either. Jasmin and James had a little girl, Sarah.

The table was lively with conversation with family jokes only understood by the Nolan-clan. In a brief moment of rare silence, Nathanial blurted out, "I'm gay."

The table grew even quieter. Half of us looked down at our plates while the other half looked around in search of the right answer to say. Suddenly, James Jr. said ,"We know, bro. It's no big deal so eat." That was James — to the point and matter-of-fact.

"What?" asked Nathanial.

"We know!" he repeated. Nathanial scanned the table and saw his other brothers nod in casual agreement with approving smiles sent his way.

"How?" Nathanial asked inquisitively.

"Look, bro, you are the sensitive one. Remember when you felt bad for the GI Joe figure that got decapitated? Remember the flowered shirt you wanted rather than the plaid we all picked for Easter. No surprise. Go with it".

The table was quiet again because the one person Nathanial needed to hear from was silent. "Dad?", he asked. Another pause but then what I would have expected to happen eventually happened.

"Nathanial, my world changed. My view of the real world changed with your sister's ...(pause). I learned that my children are gifts from God. *You* are my gift from God. I don't know anything else except that I want all of you to be healthy and happy, in whatever you chose," Dad said with a sniffle. "Now, would someone pass the sweet potatoes? A man could starve in this family".

And at that, the conversation and laughter broke out again and continued right through to pumpkin pie.

———————

Our wedding came off without a hiccup. To test Dad's resolve that he just wanted his children to be happy, Perry and I bravely told him we didn't want a religious church wedding, and only wanted an officiant guiding the ceremony. We had prepared rituals that were meaningful to us, intermingled with tradition. "Daughter," he said with authority, "I *will* perform your wedding. Period. End of discussion. But I will do it your way, even if it is a heathen ceremony," he said smiling.

So, on August 14th, Nathanial led the wedding procession dressed dashingly in a tuxedo, followed by the bridesmaids. Perry, Byron, Troy and the groomsmen were standing up front. Dad walked me down the aisle toward the front. He handed Perry my arm and proceeded to where Mom was standing. Perry and I turned to the guests and Nathanial said,

"Who gives this woman to be married?"

"We do, in love and promise," was my parents' in-unison response.

Mom sat back down, and Dad took his place as the officiator. Instead of lighting a unity candle we lit a stock of sage that was sitting in a large mother-of-pearl shell. Instead of a traditional religious ceremony we carried the proceedings ourselves with vows, promises, humor, and love. We did allow Dad to pronounce us *Husband and Wife, friends forever.* We left the altar area, Byron between us, to the song *Let Your Love Fly* by The Bellamy Brothers.

After the reception had been going lively for two hours, Mom grabbed my arm and led me into her bedroom where Grandma Jane had already arrived. On the bed lay two beautifully wrapped gifts.

"Amelia, we each have a special gift for you on this special day." Mom picked up the book-size present and put it in my hands. I unwrapped it carefully; my mind was racing and wondering what could be so precious to give it to me in private? With the silver wrapping off, I stared at the small tattered journal in my hands and opened the cloth cover gently. Inside the worn cover ,were the barely legible words, *Madame Frances Jane Blayney's Diary*. It was in her handwriting, I was certain. "I found it in a trunk Aunt Lucy had in her attic", Mom explained. Aunt Lucy was Grandma Jane's sister and passed away last Summer. "I decided to give it to you as a wedding gift."

Tears welled in my eyes and I thanked her. Before I could say anything else, Grandma Jane took the book and put it on the bed. She replaced it with a small square box. Inside the box was a round locket. I opened the locket and what stared back at me was an old photograph of Fanny to the right and on the left a current picture of me. "There's a connection between you two, so I thought you should have Frances' locket".

I sat tentatively down on the bed, holding the pendant and the journal in my lap. I was deeply moved by the thoughtfulness of the gifts but there was something more intense moving inside me. There was uneasiness within me, and these items so intimately connected with my Great Grandmother. What was it? I sensed there was something unsaid — something untold.

Looking up, I glanced at Grandma Jane for any clues as to what I was sensing.. Her sweet gaze showed only love and peace. Then I looked to Mom who seemed nervous although she did not show it on the outside — I sensed it within her. Without thought, I broke the moment of silence.

"Mom, there's something you haven't told me." With that, she looked away and her far away glare was now clear to both Grandma Jane and I. "You've never shared your own cross-over experience. You know, when your hair is down. Grandma says you have it, too, but I don't know anything about them.

In her defense, and typical of a mother's protective mode, Grandma chimed in immediately. "Amelia, this is your big day. We need to get back out to the reception. I'll bet Perry is looking for you".

I was not to be dissuaded from my mission. With Grandma's apparent dismissal of my question, and Mom's clear avoidance of my eyes, I could not leave the room without an answer…big day or not.

"Amelia," Mom said, "I will tell you but not now, not today. I promise. Soon, ok?"

"Is it bad?" I asked, not able to let it go so quickly.

"It's complicated," was her small offering.

"No." I quipped. "Not good enough. Maybe we don't have the time now to hear a big long story, but you can't leave me hanging. Give me something. I'm not leaving this room until you do!" my voice escalating.

Mom looked at Grandma and said nothing. "*A leahb*, You and I see our ancestors in another time and space."

"Yes…" I egged on.

"Your Mother sees visions of the future. It's different than our gift".

"And…?" I urged not, not letting the answer get away.

"Stop it!" cried Mom. "That's enough!"

Knowing I wouldn't give up or let this go, Grandma had the final say before she took my arm and led me back to the party.

"Your Mother thinks she saw your death, Amelia. Now, how about some cake?"

7

'Twas so cold

From the bedroom, I re-entered the wedding celebration of cutting the cake, the first dance as a married couple and throwing the bouquet. At first, all I could think about were the words Grandma whispered to me as we left the bedroom; *"Leave it alone, Amelia."*

I wasn't even sure what she meant but it was unsettling. Still, Perry was so handsome in his tux and I was wearing a beautiful white gown with beaded lace — and this was my wedding day! Soon, I fell into the gaiety of the reception and temporarily forgot the conversation with Mom and Grandma Jane.

The father-daughter dance was lovely as was my dance with Nathanial. I was the belle of the ball and all my favorite people were celebrating with me. Byron was running around chasing an older child, falling on the ground in great waves of laughter. His three-year old laugh was infectious.

Perry and I, even from across the room, stole glances at each other in a promise of a lifetime of love. Our wedding theme was *Love Blossoms,* with sparkling white lights streaming

78

overhead and crystal lit candles on each table. It all created an atmosphere of romance. Perry and I had re-entered the reception area with flower blossom falling on us as Nathanial announced, "Let me be the first to introduce Amelia O'Malley-Nolan and Perry Joseph Driscoll as husband and wife."

The guests clapped as we danced into the reception. It had not gone unnoticed that Nathanial hadn't introduced us as Mr. & Mrs. Perry Driscoll. I could only be an O'Malley-Nolan. While Perry resisted the idea that I wouldn't be taking his last name as my own, I didn't give him an opportunity for a vote. Driscoll was a perfectly wonderful Welsh name, but it wasn't my name. I wouldn't lose my identity because of a silly custom. The importance of the O'Malley-Nolan was heightened for me because of the cross-overs with Fanny.

Our honeymoon was short but very romantic. Both of our parents pitched in and bought us four days and nights at a resort on Orcas Island, north-west of Seattle. To get to the island, we took the three-hour ferry boat trip across the San Juan Straits. We hiked during the day, as weather permitted, or stayed cozy in our suite during the two days it rained, ordering room service for our breakfast and lunch but venturing out each night for a quiet dinner. Our lovemaking was awkward on our wedding night, but we fell into a sweet union after that.

When we returned from the honeymoon, our hurried lives quickly resumed. I planned to start college the following fall but Perry started classes just two weeks after we returned hone from our honeymoon. We moved into our married student housing basement apartment and enrolled Byron at the college preschool.

I had time to furnish the apartment with gifts from our parent's attics. Grandma donated her spare bedroom set so that we would have a bed right away. I found dishes, pots and pans, and all the necessities for a kitchen where neither of us knew how to cook. It would be an adjustment for us both.

It took only three weeks to have our apartment livable and comfortable. Now, I had another 11 months on my hands before starting college. I returned to my job working Monday through Thursday but with Perry gone between his part-time job and his classes, I had time to think. The hustle and bustle of the wedding and settling into the apartment, had left me little time to think about the conversation with Grandma Jane and Mom on my wedding day. Now, I had time and it became increasingly necessary to hear the whole story.

In early October, I called Mom on the phone, under the guise of finalizing plans for Dad's birthday dinner and cake. In 1975, Dad had left the church as pastor, to co-found a not-for-profit service helping unwed mothers with the emotion, spiritual and physical challenges of having a baby. Most of the women he helped, through "Fresh Starts," had been shunned by family and left to deal with their pregnancy on their own. Dad had worked very hard on starting this enterprise, and he worked tirelessly to get it to the success it had become in just a year. For this reason, we wanted his birthday to be extra-special. It was also was a milestone, because he would be turning 60.

After we had spoken for about 30 minutes, securing all the details of the birthday celebration, I turned the conversation my direction. "Mom, it's time you tell me the story of your cross-overs and why it's been so secretive."

"Amelia, I don't want to get into that now," was her immediate response, nearly cutting me off to get it said.

"Ok, then, when?" I asked patiently.

"Soon, dear, but there's really little to tell, so don't you worry about it. You have enough on your plate with being a new bride and taking care of Byron. By the way, is he still coming over on Saturday so you and Perry can run your errands?" she cleverly added to change the subject.

By mid -November, I asked her two other times to tell me the story of her crossover stories, and each time she would give me the same brush-off and redirect the conversation. Frustrated, but not deterred, I made another tea-date with Grandma Jane.

As usual, entering into Grandma Jane's home was a retreat from the world. Always warmer than we kept our basement apartment, I was instantly relaxed and at peace sitting down at the kitchen table. Water was boiling for our tea, and Grandma Jane was slicing me a large piece of coconut cake with cream-cheese frosting. "This is Mabel's recipe. She got it out of Reader's Digest. I hope it's good," she said as she cut her a piece, too. I knew it would be good because Grandma couldn't bake anything else. My first bite proved that theory to be correct. It melted in my mouth, and in that moment, I couldn't remember anything tasting as good. The tea was exceptional that day, as well. Grandma didn't just have milk to put in the tea — she always had cream. Tea with cream and sugar was practically like its own dessert.

"Would you like another piece? You've lost weight, Amelia. I need to fatten you up!" she said with a smile. She was right, I had lost weight since my wedding. I was struggling to learn how to cook, and most of the casseroles I attempted ended in crusty tops and burnt bottoms. The joke in our apartment-home was this:

Step 1. Aggressively plunge the spoon into the top of the casserole to break the hard crust. If you didn't break the crust, the spoon would likely bounce off and hit the person next to you.

Step 2. Carefully put the serving spoon in just deep enough to scoop out the middle mixture, avoiding the black charcoal mess at the bottom.

Step 3. No matter what, tell mom it's great. Step 4. Always make sure there's bread and butter on the table to supplement the casserole — that was uneatable. We labeled this, "The rules of the Casserole."

I declined a second piece of coconut cake but accepted the refill of my hot tea. When there was a lull in our reminiscing of the wedding, the list of gifts received, and Byron's upcoming fourth birthday party, I approached the real reason I had asked to come over. "Grandma, I need to know why Mom is so secretive about her crossover experiences. What is it that is not being said?"

"I think that's for your mother to tell you, Amelia," she kindly replied.

"I know, but she won't. I've asked three times, and she won't!"

"Be patient. It's a difficult story for your mom. Be patient, *A Leanhb.*"

"Grandma, you and I, see our ancestors, in our visions, set in their time and in what we think is an actual event that's going on. It doesn't appear they even know we're there. Is Mom's vision different?" I pushed.

Grandma looked at me, paused and continued. "This isn't a hard science, Amelia. There are many versions of it, I'm sure. I've read about people that have conversations with spirits as if they *are* really there and still others that see the future. I saw on television last night, how one lady helps the police solve crimes by using her special abilities. I don't know how that works, but I'm grateful I don't have that gift."

I read between the lines. Grandma was not going to tell Mom's story, but she was telling me that Mom's gift included seeing future events. While Grandma cleared the kitchen table, I thought about how scary that might be to see the future, especially if something bad was to happen. But then something else occurred to me. "Grandma, Did Mom see my near drowning in a vision?"

Another long pause, "Yes, Amelia," was the limit to her response and at that she restarted planning Byron's party, firmly sending me a message that she would say no more.

Before leaving, I bravely asked one more question. "Grandma, have you read your mother's journal? You know, the one Mom gave to me on my wedding day?"

"You haven't?" she quizzed.

"No. It's been so busy since the wedding, and everything," I confessed. "Have you?" I asked again.

"Yes, Amelia, I have read it and you should too. I think it will help you understand." And, at that, I kissed her cheek and went home to find the journal.

Octover 4, 1867. 'Twas a gloomy day as twas most days, and me walk to the lake twas slow. Da told his bans of the plans to marry ms reid. Ma had only been takin a year sinc. How cud he?

Me life 'twas nothin. He wud have me cook and clene for 9 bairns with nary a thoht for me. I can not do it. I stod on the brokin wood doc and saw the water was cod and dark. I sae the water as me Ma, invitin me in. It was just one step.

It was cod. I wnt under. I did not have a dublin-care. The dark sky was me heart and the cod water me life. 'Twas in a momint that the sky openind and I sae lit. The water warmd me and Ma came to me not az a gost but in me mind. I memberd her smil and loov. She tod me to go bac and be strong. I was under the water dep and me dress was lik a ston. I foht to get bac up. I wod liv and fur me Ma and fur her. Chad puld me out and we went hom. 'Twas not spokn of sinc.

I reread this diary entry three times to grasp its meaning partly because of the poor English writing but mostly because I could have been the one writing it, too.

The water was turning cold for me but warm for her — the skies bright for me then switching to dark while it was the opposite for her. It was so emotionally charged — reading like a suicide note.

The dress *like a stone*. Yes. It was the dress there, too, for me. It was Fanny's dress but I had it on. I didn't know how to reconcile this, but there it was in writing. Her writing. I knew my great-grandmother was born in 1855, so at this writing she was 12, just one year after her mother had died.

The entries before this one were sparse and filled with *"we had no fod toda. Ma bold a potato and we shard. I hugry and the bairns to."* It seems that food was in short supply and other entries mentioned having the one dress that would remain dirty, because it was too cold to remove to be washed and dried in front of the fire. She entioned that the tub for washing had frozen up and, for several day, they had no way to wash. These entries, in her diary, were every-day details and heartbreaking. There were other hardships as well:

Summer 1866, "Ma tod us her cusins Mary and Darn ded at sea comin to see us."

Between the entries of her Ma boiling one potato to be shared by 9 children, until the October entry that her jumping into the lake, there was no account on how Lucinda O'Malley died. Perhaps starvation?

But she does write about her father's wedding to Jane Reid as a big party with food, dancing and music. The community chipped in with home-baked goods and the fiddler. She later wrote an entry dated 1869, that Ma Jane was teaching her how to read and write "proper." From then on, the journaling was easier to read.

"Decembr 1870 'Twas Amelia's birth day today. Ma Jane cookd a cake, and it was good. The little ones love Ma Jane" and another entry; *"Ma Jane had a baby* ~~agin~~ *again. Pansy we call her."*

An entry dated February 1880, told of her own marriage to Henry O'Malley and how marrying Henry was like marrying a brother, since the two families were so close. Still, she wrote it was a good thing to marry and create a home of her own. It also included the sad tale of how their first born accidentally drown in that same lake where Fanny had once considered ending her life. Because these entries elicited deep emotional turmoil for me, I quit reading after this 1880 entry.

I put the diary on a shelf in a hall linen closet where it remained until we moved to California six years later. Then it was transferred to a box labeled "misc" and put into an attic in our new home. It wouldn't be until the summer of 2005 that I would pull it back out and begin reading again.

Life took on a different flavor from the fall of 1977 through my Bachelor of Psychology's completion in 1980. I took 20 credits, most terms except during the summer when only took 12. I was able to quit my job because Perry had completed his bachelor's, the year prior, and secured an excellent part-time job, making the stress of my paid position more trouble than it was worth financially. This made the total immersion into my academics more plausible toward success.

A Bachelor in Psychology meant very little in a financial sense, but it was where my passion was and I immediately applied for and was accepted into the Master's program. Perry did the same, starting an MBA program.

Between the two of us, our stacks of books out numbered any other item in the apartment. Furniture remained minimal so books became end tables and nightstands. We had a rule about always eating dinner together even if it meant eating late .

Looking back, I think this one family agreement made our lives seem cohesive even in the midst of busyness.

My interest in pursuing psychology was not to be a counselor, but to be in a field of research. Since my dad's conflict with the "church" people, I began to wonder why groups of people banded together creating a set of rules while shunning those that don't conform. I'd been furious at the way the church treated Dad during my pregnancy but now I just wanted to understand this universal phenomena of tribalism and *I am right, You are wrong* mentality.

I would later learn that this is a common philosophy among most faith traditions. My Master' thesis was on this topic, and it won me an invitation to begin a doctorate in Berkeley, California.

In 1982, we moved to California so that I could pursue a Ph.D. Otherwise, we were the typical American family, reserving weekends toward family outings and trips back up north to visit Mom, Dad and Grandma Jane. Those short hiatus' back home, also gave Perry and I a chance for date-nights. Mom would watch Byron while Perry and I stole away for a quiet evening — just us two. Grandma Jane had moved in with Mom and Dad, mostly as a precaution to her advancing age.

Balancing the constraints of the doctorate program, while keeping a home and staying connected with family, took it's toll on me, but no one could see it from the outside — I made sure of that.

My dissertation finished in 1987 — *Tribalism and Belonging; Innate mental process in collective thought.* I immediately took a part-time teaching position at The University of California and continued the research, publishing my first book in 1988, and the second one two years later. Perry had landed a prestigious job as a financial manager, and together our lifestyle was comfortable.

With the publishing of this second book, Byron was heading off to college, beginning a Business major at California State University and following in his father's footsteps.

The empty-nest syndrome is just what they warn; with Byron out of the house and off to college, Perry and I had to re-negotiate our marriage. The first year was the toughest, and we both felt the gap in family dynamics. I was still only teaching as adjunct faculty and continuing my research while accepting a few local speaking engagements on the findings — weekends still held sacred for Perry and I to re-invent our roles.

While I sometimes mused about my childhood and the cross-over experiences, life was too busy to continue down that rabbit hole. Grandma Jane and I remained close but never spoke of the subject again, and I decided not to push my mom about her experience any further.

It's funny how you can go along for a long time in your little hamlet of work, family, friends and you are convinced you have it all. But then something throws a big wrench into the picture and life is chaos again.

Grandma Jane's death in 1990, at age 100, was during the publishing of my second book and seeing Byron off to college. Its was, also, the year when I was in demand for speaking engagements, regarding my research on Tribal Behavior. I was mechanical in keeping it all together; keeping a routine, careful not to deviate off course. When she died, I stuffed my grief down in a neat package of *business*.

The funeral was lovely and Mom had done an exceptional job capturing the essence of Jane Blayney O'Malley, in a display of her favorite things and pictures of her throughout the years. I played a minimal role in the service and planning other than helping dismantle Grandma's material possessions — boxing it all up and placing it in Mom's attic. When it was over, I was both relieved and ready to move on. I couldn't afford to come apart. Coming apart would come later.

On a Tuesday in 1992, I flew to San Diego to speak at a conference on brain science and its relationship to my research: *Tribalism and Belonging*. I had given the same speech on many occasions. While routine on the surface, this single event would be one of several — cascading to my demise.

GOING UNDER

Truly, it is in the darkness that one finds the light, so when we are in sorrow, then this light is nearest of all to us.

~Meister Eckhart

8

One Way of the Other

I arrived in San Diego with only moments to spare before the conference began. As I was waiting at my front row table a wave of unbelievable grief came over me. It was as if a brick wall was crumbling within. I started to shake uncontrollably. A woman sitting next to me noticed and said, "Nervous, dear?" I knew it wasn't nerves, but I didn't know what it was. I stood carefully suspecting that I could pass out if I rose too fast, and exited the conference room. Reaching an alcove in the central lobby area, I broke down in wails of tears. Few people were still in the lobby but two women standing nearby ran to me and half-carried me to an unoccupied smaller conference room. For 45 minutes, I cried — no I wept.

These two caring women stayed with me, offering tissue and sips of water. Never once did they suggest I calm down or leave to get help. It turned out that these women were both psychologists with a specialty in grief management. They had diagnosed my hysteria and instinctively knew what I needed in that golden-hour.

When I came up for air, my eyes were swollen and, my face red. The amount of used Kleenex could have covered a small child. My first words were, "I don't know what happened," of which one woman replied, "What happened is that a sea of grieving needed to flood out."She was right and at that moment I knew I was grieving for Grandma Jane, two years after her death. All that I had kept neatly bottled inside, could no longer be contained. "One way or another, grief will emerge, " these two began to explain. "Sometimes it bubbles over manifesting in illness and other times in self-destructive behavior, but if you're lucky, it comes in total release just in the nick of time."

———————

My return home from San Diego was uneventful on the exterior. In total exhaustion, I slept for two days. Perry came into the room, periodically, to check on me and offer sips of water and bowls of soup. On the third night, I rallied. Fully rested, we celebrated my *return* with dinner out at our favorite restaurant. Over dessert, I recounted what happened in San Diego. Perry listened compassionately, reached across the table to tenderly stroke my hand. He was silent, which I appreciated. It was not the time to offer platitudes like ,"It's for the best", or "I'm sorry you went through that." Or even sage advice by trying to fix it. The silence spoke volumes of love to me.

"I've had a few days to process this, Perry. After all, my sharp exit and missing my spot on the speaker circuit, left me with the rest of the conference to hide out in my room!" I explained.

"Perry, I've decided to leave the University to write full time. I think the emotional boil-over was long in coming and it had a cleansing effect on me. I realized, for the first time, that while I am a good professor, my love is in the research and talking about what I discover."

Perry was quiet again and I wondered if I would hear concerns about a reduction in our finances, without my adjunct teaching, or maybe he would discount my idea as a temporary bit of insanity that I would get over in time.

Instead, Perry thoughtfully said, "Amelia, I've seen this coming for a few years now. I've seen the joy when you're invited to speak about your research and I don't see that same joy as you prepare for your classes. I've seen your endless energy on the days you spend in the study working on your latest book and I've seen the total exhaustion when you return from teaching. You are a brilliant researcher and write, Amelia. I support you".

My eyes welled up with tears…tears of love for this man sitting across from me. He never ceased to surprise me. Still, Perry needed to say the next thing. "Without your steady income though, we will need to make some lifestyle changes. Byron is off at school and the house is too big for us. We don't need four bedrooms. Let's consider downsizing and creating a space for two

DINKS," Perry said in jest. I had heard that acronym before: Double Income -No Kids.

I loved our home. We had only been there for five years, buying it just as I finished the Ph.D. and a few years before Grandma Jane's death. I had spent those five years decorating it and staying very engaged in its creation.

At age 37, I didn't like the idea of leaving what was so carefully put together, or the idea of starting over, but I knew he was right, and I knew that a change would be good medicine for me. Even in my reservations, I understood that Perry was giving me a mile of understanding. Going along with his desire to live a simpler lifestyle was a small price to pay — to carry out this vision for the rest of my career.

From the time we put our home on the real estate market, until we received a full-price offer, was exactly five days. The transition was smooth but very busy. I had resigned my teaching position on Monday, after our decision to down-size, and that set the ball in motion. Packing up and moving was physically challenging for both Perry and I, but Byron came home for a long weekend and helped. He had grown into a tall and handsome young man, and we appreciated the youthful muscles!

Samuel was now working as an IT geek in Silicon Valley, and he volunteered his moving skills, as well. To save money, we rented a 27 foot rental truck and loaded it three times before the house was empty. Two of the loads went to our new place, and the third load went to a charity thrift shop. We felt good about releasing our overflow of possessions and giving them away, rather than selling them.

We sold our four bedroom home and purchased a two bedroom condo. By the end of the moving day, we were all exhausted, but I seemed to have taken the most significant blow of complete body failure.

Every muscle in my body ached, and I vowed, out loud, to never move again. With boxes and furniture hastily placed, I collapsed, too tired to even eat the pizza we purchased as a dinner reward for our hard work. Byron and Samuel quickly left after pizza and beer, leaving Perry and me to take in this enormous life-changing venture. Perry said it first, "Did we do the right thing?"

"I don't know," I said, "but we're here now, and if I have to move one more muscle, I'll die."

Perry had to be at work that Monday and the unpacking of boxes, was my only job now. I was very good at organizing such an undertaking and within three days, our living space resembled a smaller version of our life in the big house. In fact, I was at my best when I had job to do, rather than thinking about it. I could spend hours over books and professional journals, without remembering to eat. I think it's safe to say, that I was at my best when I was busy. I didn't do well at relaxing or having nothing to do.

In the organization of our new home, I stayed busy from 8 a.m. until the time Perry came home from work, about 7 p.m. My breaks were minimal — something to eat, a cup of coffee or checking any phone messages on our new answering machine. When I was not fully done setting up our home, after two days, I put in extra energy the third day, to ensure I would finish the job.

Perry was much the same personality except that he had a few hobbies like fly-fishing or preparing tax returns for friends. Together our home remained well maintained and cared for as did our car (well, that was Perry's territory). We were working-machines and enjoyed weekends putting paint on the walls or cleaning out the outside gutters. When there was nothing much to do at home, we took off on a day road trip visiting wineries or a museum. From breakfast until after dinner we were busy. This was the life we had established and grown into. There was a sense of sweet, quiet contentment, which included our intimate lives in the bedroom. Perry was always gentle, kind and considerate in our lovemaking. We didn't need to vary our sexual lives because it was fine the way it was.

Two weeks after we had moved into our new condo, I went to bed early with a book. Perry came in with the expected, "Are you ok? I thought we were going to work on the budget?"

The truth was, I didn't want to work on the budget. That was Perry's job, because that was his special talent. I had little interest in numbers, other than statistics of how many people followed their religious leader's teachings, without question. We had never had a budget before, and if Perry felt it was necessary, I was sure it was — but I didn't need to be involved.

"Just let me know when you're finished with it, and I'll look it over. I'm sure it will be fine," I answered without lifting my eyes from the book. That seemed fine to Perry. I imagined it was how he preferred it anyway, since it came so easy to him. I knew how much he made from his management job, and how little I brought to the table. I knew our major expenses, and it didn't take a financial wizard to understand our spending would need to be carefully watched. I trusted Perry would be accurate, fair and generous. Period. I was done thinking about it. Within 10 minutes of reading the boring novel in my lap, I fell asleep. Or, at least I thought I was asleep.

"Amelia, Amelia, wake up," I heard a familiar female voice. I opened my eyes to see my great grandmother, Frances, looking right at me, standing at the side of the bed. "You have to tell Byron. You have to tell him. Tell him soon." At that she walked out of the bedroom. I quickly followed, only to find the hallway empty.

"What the hell?" I said quietly out loud. Going back to bed, I did a mental weighing of two possibilities: Either it was Fanny, but she was not talking to me — but to her sister Amelia, or she *was* talking to me, and this visit was different than the others.

I felt the back of my head and confirmed my hair was still up in a small ponytail. I had cut my hair a year ago into a shoulder length bob-cut but still wore it back off of my face most of the time. Nothing was the same as the other cross-overs. "It must have been a dream," I thought.

Still, I continued to process it as if it were real. *Tell Byron what?* If Fanny was talking to her sister, Amelia, what was it she was to tell her nephew, Byron? If not, what was *I* supposed to tell my Byron?

I reached for the phone to call Grandma Jane, then remembered she was no longer available to me. My eyes fill up with tears, as I laid back down on my pillow. The bedside light was still on and had been throughout the *dream* state. It took a long time to fall back asleep, but when I awoke, again, the bedroom lights were off and Perry was snoring next to me.

While looking around the darkened room, the image of Grandma Jane was before me. She was solid, not a ghostly figure, but she seemed to come from nowhere. "*A leanbh*, tell Byron. He needs to know."

In a whisper so as not to wake Perry, I replied in frustration, "Tell him what!"

"He needs to hear the story, his story," was her simple reply. At that, she left the bedroom.

"Damn!" I said as I jumped out of bed to follow her. Expecting to find the hall empty, I was startled to see her slowly walking away. She turned toward me.

"Tell him, Amelia. Tell him his story," and then she was gone.

It's a common understanding that mothers have a sixth sense about their children. Mothers know when something is wrong — instinctively. I didn't have that. I loved Byron very much but I had no idea that he needed something from me. The next day, after Grandma Jane and her mother visited me in the bedroom, I called Byron. Still, without a clue to what I should tell him, I uncharacteristically decided to wing it.

Byron was sharing a small home near his school. His roommate, Nick, was a great find on a local bulletin-board on campus. They shared the 1927 two bedroom bungalow as well as the single phone with an answering machine. The phone rang four times before the machine kicked in. *Hi, if you're trying to reach Byron or Nick you made it. Leave a message at the beep.*

I didn't want to leave a message that might alarm Byron, so I put on my best happy-mom voice and told him to call me when he could. Byron lived 45 minutes away from Perry and I, but highly involved in his studies as well as having an active social life. When he did not return my call that day, I didn't worry.

When he didn't call the next day, I knew something was up. Careful not to jump to conclusions, I decided to just drive down to see him. The new condo was put together and I was waiting for the delivery of two academic journals, to begin a section of my latest research, which allowed me plenty of time to check on Byron.

I left the house at 8 a.m. I knew he started classes at 11 a.m., so I had hoped to catch him before his day began. Arriving just before 9 a.m., I knocked on the door. Ready to greet Byron with a motherly hug, his roommate, Nick, answered the door instead.

"Hi, Nick," I said a bit startled. We had met Nick twice before. He was an artist majoring in Fine Arts, while working at a pet shop. The last we had heard, Nick worked the early shift at the pet store and then went to class, so I was surprised to see him there.

"Hi, Ame, I mean Mrs. Nolan." I didn't correct him. I wasn't Mrs. anything really. Keeping my name and not changing Byron's name to Driscoll was confusing to most. I left it alone.

"I need to see Byron. Is he in?" Nick hesitated and an invitation to come into the house, still not offered.

"Sure," he said after a moment, stepping aside to allow me entrance. I thought to myself that his behavior was odd. Nick should not even be there, and he was not eager to have me come in.

"Nick, you are acting odd. What's up and where is Byron? I left a message for him two days ago and he hasn't returned my call."

"Mrs. Nolan, Byron is in his room. He's been sick...I mean he's not been feeling well."

"What does he have, the flu?" I said seeking clarification.

"No, not the flu," Nick said in hesitation.

"OK, Nick, just tell me. I'm about to walk in there to see him, and I need more information. You have that information, and I need for you to tell me right now."

Nick sat down on a metal and vinyl kitchen chair and I sat on the other. "I think Byron should tell you the whole thing, but last weekend he started having hallucinations and freaking out. I took him to the emergency room, and he was put on some anti-psychotic meds."

"Hallucinations? Like what?" I quipped.

"Maybe he should tell you, Mrs. Nolan. I should get ready for work now." At that, Nick stood up and walked to the hallway bathroom and shut the door. Shortly after that, I heard the shower turn on.

Stunned and shaken, I slowly made it down to Byron's bedroom door. It was shut, and all seemed quiet inside. I knocked softly, with no response. I knocked again, with a bit more intent and called out his name. I heard a soft voice call me in.

Sitting up in bed was a red-eyed young man with nervous hands. I entered and sat on the edge of the bed. Not understanding what I was seeing, I carefully reached out and quieted his hand movements. Byron gripped my hand in a desperate latch. He looked exhausted. I broke the silence. "Tell me the story," was all I said.

Over the next hour, Byron spoke of his hallucinations. On more than one occasion, he described seeing someone named Fanny and other children dancing around his bed. In another vision, he saw himself drowning and rescued by someone named Chad or Chet. He described these day-dreams as nightmares. The one that set him over the edge, was the vision of me dying in my bed. It was that nightmare that caused Nick to insist he see a doctor. Byron ended the story with a loud and exaggerated sigh, as if telling it to me was a huge relief.

"Byron, I should have told you this sooner, and for that I am sorry. What you saw was not a hallucination or a dream. It was the family gift." I told him enough about the cross-overs for his visions to have meaning. I told him who Fanny and Chadwallder were and the whole story of my near drowning at age 12 — and that of Fanny's, too. I left out an explanation about seeing my death because I had no explanation to give. "Byron, you are not crazy and you don't need medication." I then told him about my recent encounters with both Fanny and Grandma Jane that had led me here to tell him this.

Byron was quiet and then said, "Well, I don't want this! I don't deserve this! It has to stop, or I will go crazy."

"I know. We will work on that together," I comforted. "I know it's something that can be controlled.Byron." Up until last night, I firmly believed the cross overs could be controlled, but the conversations I had with those two dead ancestors were anything but controlled!

"Byron, are you able to come home for a few days?" He gave that thought and to my surprise resigned in agreement.

"I already let my professors know that I was sick and probably would miss class this week. I need to be home and I need you to fix this, Mom."We gathered his clothes and toiletries in a small grocery bag, loaded it in the car and said goodbye to Nick through his bedroom door. I left my home number on a table, in case Nick wanted to check in. The only thing left to do was head north toward home.

We were quiet as I drove across the Bay Bridge and then Byron asked, "Can I go see Grandma Jane. I mean, where she is now?"

9

Fear

Grandma Jane was buried in Tacoma, Washington, 35 miles south of Seattle. I had purchased plane tickets out of Oakland for the Tuesday after our return to the condo. Our first few days at home were intense. It was clear, this was not the same carefree young man we had sent off to college. His mood was quiet and he often stole away to the guest room.

The one meaningful connection between us occurred at the kitchen table over coffee. There he restated his desire to visit Grandma Jane's grave. While he was grateful to know more about this family "gift", he needed more information. Perhaps, if he could be in the world of his ancestors, he could wrap his head around it. It was "a shot in the dark", as he put it, but it was all he had. Seeing Byron suffer and not being able to make the pain go away was maddening.

The family gift of cross-over had shifted, and I felt I was clueless on how to help Byron understand. I needed more information, too, and I knew where to find the missing pieces — Mom. Before setting out toward the airport, I called her. The disclosure of her experience, with our ancestors was left unfinished. I didn't want to be unkind or disrespectful toward her, but I was determined, as hell, to finally get some answers.. My parents were now in their 70's, but they were active with sharp minds. I would take advantage of this while I could.

On the second ring, Mom answered the phone. "Hi, Mom. It's Amelia. How are you and Dad?" We exchanged niceties, and when I had enough of that , I just said it. "Byron is not ok. He's experienced things I cannot explain to him, but you can. We are flying up today to visit Grandma Jane and then we will be over, probably around 3. We will see you then. Goodbye Mom." I slowly returned the phone to the receiver and let out a sigh. I had given her no way to wiggle out of it, and I would no longer allow her to hide behind whatever it was that was so uncomfortable for her. I was a mom myself now, and in protection mode. The bear cub was in danger, and I was the fightin' momma bear.

The flight north was smooth and uneventful. Byron spoke a little about his studies, and his desire to have his own business one day. He talked about liking a particular professor, and how the professor encouraged Byron to think big — beyond the previous achievements of others. It was an emotional relief to have a conversation with Byron about his academics, and a good sign that his mind continued to search for normalcy. Byron wasn't mentally ill; he was mentally confused, having experienced something he could not package neatly. Knowing who Fanny and Chad were seemed to help him begin the process of acceptance rather than remain in a state of fear.

Through my research on societal psychology, I found over and over again the damage that fear plays on an individual's mental well-being. Fear can be a link to our poor behavior and quietly erodes the spirit and common sense. Fear is useful when you need to run from a tiger but otherwise, it usually causes harm.

I told Byron about my plan. We would land at SeaTac airport, rent a car and drive to Tacoma, directly to the cemetery, and I would give him all the time he needed there. I would remain in the car, a street away from where Grandma Jane lay. When he was ready, we would leave and have a nice quiet lunch at our favorite Thai cafe. Next, we would go see Nana Voada because she would be able to shed more understanding to what he had encountered. He seemed agreeable to the three-stop plan, although his demeanor remained reserved and he continued in his thoughts. When we were not talking he looked out the window of the car and drifted off.

Grandma Jane's grave was under a large pine tree, in the New Tacoma Cemetery. She was next to Grandpa Frank. There were two un-occupied, un-scripted grave markers, on either side of them, which were intended for Mom and Dad. Michael, Henry, and Patrick, Mom's siblings, lived out of state and rarely returned to the Seattle/Tacoma area of their childhood. Mom was the only child ,of Grandma Jane and Grandpa Frank, that remained nearby.

It was unsettling to see those empty plots, although we never spoke of it after Grandpa Frank's death so many years ago. Grandpa Frank purchased all four grave sites at the same time during a sale promotion by the cemetery's new owner. Creepy... but thrifty.

As we drove into the cemetery, I mentioned to Byron that I had brought a small throw blanket if he wanted to take it and sit at her grave. The ground was always predictably soggy in the Pacific Northwest. He accepted. Slowly, I drove the car to the spot where she lay. Getting out of the car to retrieve the blanket, I couldn't help but notice that Byron had not budged. I shut the trunk lid, and it seemed to startle him out of his solitary thoughts. He opened the car door and we walked to her grave site. He stood for a moment, gazing down at her marker;

Jane Frances O'Malley Baur

b. January 26th, 1890 d. January 29th, 1990

May You Always Have Tea Beside The Fire

Grandma Jane had not asked for anything more than her name, birth, and death dates on her grave stone. My brothers and I chose the saying.

I laid out the blanket for Byron and walked away. I drove to a spot near the main building ,but a short distance for Byron to walk once he finished. Forty-five minutes later, he returned to the car. We sat in silence for a minute before he said, "That was good. She told me it would be ok". I wasn't sure what to make of that, but thought it best not to question. "I think a nice cup of hot tea would do us both a world of good!" I kindly said, and at that, we drove to lunch.

Our time together at lunch was warming. We chatted without care and ate chicken curry like starving orphans. Just before paying the bill he asked: "Mom, what is it exactly Nana will be telling us?" I told him what I knew and what I heard on my wedding day. "You mean, for 15 plus years you never asked what she meant by *she saw your death*?"

"I tried many times, but she refused to explain. I guess I didn't care that much since Grandma Jane didn't seem all that concerned either."

"Well," Byron said quickly, "I care!"

We arrived at my parent's home at 3:33, just a bit later than I had predicted. Mom was waiting at the door with smiles and hugs, eagerly helping us off with our coats. "I'll make tea and Byron can tell me all about his studies. Is there a girl for you, Byron?" We looked at each other in an acknowledgment that this was not going to be an easy.

"Let's sit in the kitchen, Mom," I said, walking to the sunlight atrium where a round- oak kitchenette table and padded chairs stood. It was a cozy room with flowered curtains and matching seat cushions. Mom busily put a pot of water on the stove and prepared three mugs of tea. She returned with tea and a plate of butter-biscuit cookies and a nervous grin on her face. She paused a moment and then sat down.

"Amelia, it's not a good idea to get into this right now. Let's enjoy Byron's visit, shall we?"

"No, Mom, we shan't," I said with sarcasm. "Byron needs you now, and frankly, I'm a bit irritated it has come to this. You should have told me the story a long time ago, and we are not leaving until you do. I know it's uncomfortable for you, but I'm not giving you a choice this time". There was another long pause and tension around the table. Our teas had gone untouched as we waited.

"Ok, Amelia, you don't have to take that tone with me". Clearing her throat, she began. "At first, I had the same crossing-over visions that you and your Grandma Jane had. I actually enjoyed them. Once, when I was 11, I played with children I didn't know — in my vision that is, although it wasn't like they knew I was there. Still, it was fun." She stopped and looked at her lap.

"Go on, Mom," I prodded.

"Then, when I was pregnant with Nathanial, I had a nightmare, but it wasn't a dream. In the vision, I was at the ocean and the sand was white, and the sun bright and warm. I was alone there, standing near the ocean's edge until a child was carried out of the water by a man. She was pale and limp. The man carrying her said, *"I'm so sorry, ma'am."* I knew, in this vision, that it was my child he was carrying. Then, my Grandmother Frances, was standing beside me. She didn't interact with me but began to weep and crumpled to the ground, muttering something I didn't understand. The pain of this vision was so intense I screamed 'NO', and it stopped."

"So, Mom, you're saying that you saw the events of my near drowning?

"Yes," was all she replied.

"But, I didn't die, Mom."

"You didn't die because I was so hysterical, remembering this vision when you went into the water, that it drew attention to the beach lifeguard, and he immediately went in after you," she said with voice escalating to prove her point.

Everyone paused in thought. "Nana, maybe this vision was a premonition, and it saved Mom's life. Isn't that a good thing?" She didn't answer.

"What else, Mom. There's more, isn't there?" I asked.

"Yes. I've had another vision since."

"...And..." I probed.

"Byron dies on a train." She whispered.

It was not what I expected but certainly appreciated: Byron laughed out loud at the notion that he would die on a train. Byron had gone from being "freaked out", to what seemed to be total acceptance now.

"I hate trains, Nana," he said through fits of laughter. Mom sat still staring off and I joined in with the giggling. It was contagious. Just then, Dad returned home from the Center and stood observing the three of us. By now, Mom had cracked and was participating in our silliness. "What's going on?" Dad said with a smile. We all just continued to laugh for a few more moments before settling into an exhausted silence.

"Hi Grandpa," Byron said as he rose to give him a big hug.

Dad sat down with us while Mom fetched him his tea. I proceeded to recount the reason for our visit and to catch him up to the present moment. I ended with, "Do you think we are crazy, Dad?"

"Here's what I think," Dad started. "I've watched, through the years, the cross-over dream with your Mom, you, Amelia, and Grandma Jane. Oh, and now Byron. As someone on the outside looking in, it seems to me that all of these visions have little to do with you. It seems, it is some replay of events long ago, and for reasons I can't explain, they present themselves in present time because of some similarities — not predictions."

"But, Jim, what about the vision of Amelia's drowning?" Mom chimed.

"Voada, did she die? And wasn't there Grandma Fanny beside you mysteriously through it? Didn't you later uncover that she'd lost an infant girl to a drowning?" At this, Mom paused and appeared to be in thought.

"I would guess, if you dug some more into the family past, you'd probably find the answers to the latest visions." I don't think you're a fortune teller, Voada. I think you have a special gift of perceiving the pain of others. Strangely, it happens to be people that are dead!" With that, we all started laughing again, ending with each of us letting out a big sigh which elicited another round of laughter. "Byron, welcome to the family of weirdness!" Dad quipped with a broad smile.

"Jim, why are you just now speaking up about this? I've held this bad feeling for months about Byron," Mom scolded.

"You didn't ask," was all Dad said, and at that, he rose from the table to refill his tea.

Byron and I flew back to California the next day. The air that begun as thick and tense was now light and airy, and more natural to breath. Byron and I talked about the visions in generalities; "When it's scary, what do you do, Mom?" I explained that we could control it, stop it at any time, and choose whether to see it in fear or something merely unexplainable. It was true that I had both purposely brought on the visions, with the release of my hair, as well as ending visions at my command.

"If you want, Byron, we can do further research into our past to see what some of this means," I offered. He declined, saying he was ready to get back to school and restart his life. I couldn't argue with that, and I thought to myself how proud I was of him for choosing to leave things unexplained, but also abandoning the fear that once paralyzed him.

Life did go on once I dropped Byron back off at his home in San Francisco, and I returned home to Perry. I resumed my daily routine of research and writing, and Perry continued to leave every morning for work. Byron completed his Bachelor's and went straight into his MBA, graduating with honors. With a Master's in Business Administration, Byron did as he had initially promised, thinking outside the box as his professor had taught him. Byron began to create his own enterprise. Perry and I invested in his start-up capital, and Byron worked long hours toward its success.

In 2001, at age 28, Byron married Parisa, a young lady he had been dating since the last year of his undergraduate program. Parisa was of Persian family descent. Her grandparents immigrating in the early 1900's. She had olive skin and long, silky, dark hair with shining eyes. She was exotic in appearance with a personality to match.

Parisa's advanced degree was in textiles. She was an artist and wildly creative in her area of expertise. It was with her unique talent ,and Byron's genius in the business world, that the two joined forces to build an export business, procuring fabric for hotels abroad. We all loved Parisa and welcomed her full-heartedly into the O'Malley -Nolan -Driscoll family.

I had once again set up my life perfectly; Byron married and with a career of his own, Perry and I in empty-nester-bliss…. So, what was this thing that was so unsettling within me? Why was I certain my perfect world was about to be challenged? Did I now have Mom's "special gift" of seeing the future?

Most importantly, could I survive what was coming next? My feelings of dread coincided with the on start of menopause. "That's it", I justified. It's just my waning estrogen! The beginnings of heat-surges and physical body changes would leave anyone on edge, I soothed myself. But along with the mature-woman changes, I was reminded that I had experienced a lot of life, and was wiser and more intuitive for it. This uneasiness meant something besides hormone bullying.

10

Happens in Fives

You know how they say that things; usually bad, happen in threes? What if, instead of three major events, five happened in a short period of time? Could a normal human being survive such an insult of calamity? I was about to find out. My parents, my marriage and my essence was about to be tested in the fires.

Life shifts are historical things you do not want or invite but ultimately change your life -path in the direction it was meant to travel, except that you did not know it.

In general, people do not like change. We want status quo and we love things we can predict. Some personalities, elicit change just for the sake of experiencing the next adventure. These people are one percent of the population. The other 99 percent hate change and avoid it at all costs…except when it is a change of delight. It's also true that there's usually a calm before the storm hits.

In 2003, Byron and Parisa had a baby girl they called Franki. They hadn't intended to have a baby so soon after they married, but sometimes life has other plans. The news that they would soon be parents was scary at first. Both were only children and had never been around babies. Their business was progressing well, and Parisa's pregnancy had the potential to slow the progress down.

While Byron was spending 70 hours a week on the company, Parisa worked part-time at an upper-end boutique, as a personal concierge for well-to-do fashionistas. Women from as far away as Los Angelas would frequent the boutique, or they would fly Parisa down for clothing and accessory consultations. Parisa had an eye for combining fabrics and adding dimension with accessories. This income kept the daily finances. The pregnancy would, for at least the last few months of pregnancy, eliminate her ability to fly. Byron had been working out of an office in an business-incubator complex, giving new start-up businesses access to small office space, shared fax machines and the internet. To save money, Byron moved his business back home and doubled to care for their new infant, so Parisa could go back to work. She hated leaving her newborn, but was also entirely dedicated to financially contributing toward the business' success.

The birth of Franki was not one of those five- things that would disrupt my world, but she was the calm that could soften the blows.

Dad turned 88 in 2004. His periodical forgetfulness was, up until then, just a family joke. We would laugh about how he left the milk in the pantry and cereal box in the refrigerator. He had turned the Center over to younger minds, ten years earlier, because his slower thinking process.

One day, he left home saying he was going up to the hardware store for light bulbs. Two hours later, he still had not arrived back home. Worried, but not sure what to do, Mom waited and hoped someone would call. As it were, a shopkeeper in midtown called the police who then called Mom. Dad was sitting on a curb on a busy intersection, she was told. Mom herself had stopped driving a few years earlier, so she hailed a cab and retrieved Dad from the corner.

He was happy to see her, but didn't appear to understand that his behavior was unusual. Dad didn't comprehend that he had driven past the hardware store, mindlessly, parking his car on an unfamiliar street and wandering. He simply sat down on the curb and seemed content to watch the traffic and pedestrians pass by.

Mom made him a medical appointment for the following week, Dad received a diagnosis of late-onset Alzheimer's.

Alzheimer's usually manifests earlier than 88. The best his doctor could explain was that he had been showing symptoms of the disease much earlier but remained functioning much longer than the textbook pattern. What my brothers and I suspected was that Mom had covered for Dad's odd behavior and there had been a steady decline in his cognitive ability for some time. It was just a few months later that Dad stopped recognizing Mom or any of his children.

We were heartbroken. This vibrant and loving man was lost somewhere in his brain. Determined that he wouldn't go into a nursing home, the six of us made a plan that Mom agreed to. The family home sold within a few months and Mom purchased a ground level two- bedroom condo in a 55 + community. While they would live independently, there was access to a licensed nurse 24 hours a day, seven days a week. The home was set up with safety features so that Dad couldn't wander off or accidentally turn on the stove and burn himself. The house was Alzheimer-proof.

The only real concern left was how this would affect Mom. Dad no longer recognized her which meant her life-long companion was gone, but still living in her home. Caregivers came in to bath him and helped move him around when he finally forget how to walk. Our plan was a good plan and the transition appeared to be working, as well as anything can work in such a horrible situation.

Number two. The phone call came in at 3 p.m. on a Tuesday in November , of the same year. Mom and Dad had been in their new place for only two months. It was one of Dad's caregivers, Emma that called me. She had come to the home, as scheduled, but no one was answering the door. She didn't work for an agency, so her point of contact was me — 1000 miles away. I knew the airline schedule well; Oakland to Seattle on flight 740 or 1301; the latter leaving in 90 minutes. It would be a total of four hours before I would arrive at the home and that wouldn't do. I instructed Emma to call the nurse hotline for assistance. In the meantime, I would be on that flight. Instinctively, I knew something was terribly wrong.

I didn't hear back from Emma by the time I boarded my plane. Anxious but staying level-headed, the trip was excruciating. Once landed and in my rental car, I called Emma repeatedly, but no one answered. Even the nurse hotline couldn't give me information other than they had dispatched a nurse to the house. I made phone calls to Uncle Michael and to James, who now lived in New York City, just to keep them in the loop.

I arrived at their condo and jumped out of the rental, seeing three police cars out front. Running up to the home, a uniformed policeman stopped me. "Ma'am, you can't go in there," she said.

"I'm their daughter!" I pleaded. The officer asked me to wait just outside the front door as she whispered something to a plain clothed officer. He came outside to talk with me. "I'm Detective Hernandez," he began. In my head, I was shouting "What the fuck is a detective doing at my parent's home!"

"I regret to inform you that your parents are gone."

"You mean they've been taken to the hospital?" I meekly asked.

"No." he said without immediate clarification. When I looked at him with a stern glare he went on. First, he guided me over to a bench, outside the condo, that Mom had placed so that she and Dad could sit and watch birds at the feeder.

"It appears your mother took your father's life and then her own. We found substance next to them that indicates suicide, but we won't know anything for sure until it's been tested." I had nowhere in my brain to hold this information. I had no speech and my body felt paralyzed. All I could think was "No, No, they must have it wrong! Mom would never do that!"

Finally, I squeaked out, "Why?" not directing the question at the detective, but out to the Universe.

"There is a note with your name on it," he said. We will give it to you once we've finished."

"Where are my parents?" I asked.

"They've already been taken to the Medical Examiners."

"For an autopsy?"

"Yes." The detective confirmed.

I had enough medical training to know that any suspicious death went to the ME for further investigation. The family's permission was not needed. Within an hour of hearing this, the police packed up and began to leave. Detective Hernandez met me back on the bench, where I had barely moved. He handed me opened envelops that had obviously been dusted for fingerprints.

"We had to open these and read them before you could have them. I'm so sorry for your loss, Ma'am. Here's my card should you have any questions."

There were three envelops with three names on them. One labeled *Michael*, one labeled *Amelia* and the third one with the unfamiliar name of *Carol* with an address in Minneapolis.

———————

Dear Amelia

    I know you won't understand this. Try not to analyze what I've done too much. I've never been as strong as you or your Dad. You did everything you could to make this work, but it couldn't ever work. All I've ever known is loving your Dad. Life without him has been unbearable. Watching him suffer from this horrible disease unacceptable, too. Please know that we did not suffer our deaths. Please explain this to your brothers and help them through it.

Love, Mom

PS Do not judge your Dad. He is a loving and wonderful man.

    I read and reread this letter several times and with each repeat, understood less and less. My mom deliberately took Dad's life and then took her own. How do you process something like that? What category of life's-lesson would this fit? I had lived 49 years, had advanced college degrees and yet, was clueless.

    I had promised to call Uncle Michael and give him an update. In my head, I rehearsed how that might go. "Hi, Uncle Mike. Hey, your sister killed my dad and then offed herself."

No, I guess not, but it reflected the anger I was feeling. How *dare* her take him away from us! How utterly selfish!

I called Uncle Michael, and in broken sentences, got the news out. On the other end there was silence at first. Then simply, "Thank you for letting me know. How are you, Amelia?" he asked mechanically.

"Fine, Uncle Michael. I'll be in touch about the funeral arrangements," and at that, we hung up. I imagined him walking away from the phone in a mindless stupor, much like I had felt after the detective told me. My next phone call was to brother James. He was the oldest and would call the other siblings. The twins and their families were now in North Carolina and Samuel, in Santa Clare. Nathanial had been *missing* for over a year now; his phone disconnected and emails unanswered. I envied him now. Nathanial would be spared, or at least delayed this trauma. With hesitation, but a little bit of familiarity now of that to say, I called James. He was an engineer with a large health care system, and I was surprised when he answered on the second ring.

"So, what's going on? How's Dad?" he immediately asked. That was James. Get to the point. He had never been one for small talk or seeing the need for niceties, if there was another purpose to a conversation. I started the story from the time I arrived at our parent's home, and ended with the words of the detective. I used his exact words; *It appears your Mother took your Father's life and then her own.* I waited for his response, but there was nothing but silence, so I went on explaining the next few hours that followed.

"I'd like you here, James. I can't do this alone." With those words, the tears flowed.

"Ok, Amelia, just stay calm. I'll get on the next plane. But I need more details."

"I don't have more details, James! The detective gave me his card to call if we have further questions. Mom left notes — three actually."

"Well, what do they say? He demanded.

"I read the one addressed to me, and it simply said she did it to save him from suffering and that she couldn't live without him." I chose not to mention the PS because I didn't want to engage in a speculative discuss on what she meant.

"And, the other two?" he asked a bit more calmly.

"One is addressed to Uncle Michael and the other to Carol Ferguson. That one has a full address and a stamp on it, ready to be mailed. The police had to open all three, I suppose for clues."

"Who's Carol?" he mindlessly asked.

"Look, James, I can't do this now. Get here when you can. I'll be at the Doubletree near the airport. Let me know when you land." I hung up nearly bursting out in tears again. My meter for patience was on empty, and I still wanted to Perry to call.

I called Perry and repeated, for the third time, how Mom had ended Dad's life before taking her own. It had only been three hours since I'd read Mom's suicide note, and every ounce of energy I had, was now reserved for staying upright. Perry would catch the next plane and be by my side soon, and for that I was grateful. Perry would let Byron know, which was a relief. Telling the story a forth time might have sent me over the edge.

I checked into the hotel, selecting the Doubletree because I was familiar with it, and because it was near the airport. Perry arrived at 11 p.m. I was so exhausted, by the time his plane landed, that he agreed to take a cab to the hotel. His eventual arrival, to our room, was instant comfort for me. I had no more tears to cry at that time, but he just held me and stroked my hair. "I'm here,", he said over and over.

At 4 a.m., Perry collected James at the airport. I had already reserved him a room at the same hotel. We embraced and I heard a whimper from James. I had never seen him cry before.

He was 14 years my senior and much of my childhood had not had him in it. He was off to college when I was too young to remember, and didn't return to live at home. He was more like a family friend than the relationship I had with my other brothers. Still, I admired him, and this embrace was a show of our kindred connection. We all sat in silence, in the hotel restaurant, drinking coffee. James broke the silence.

"I need to see them. I'd like to see the note, too." While Perry went to the room for the letter, I explained where they had taken our parents. "I've already called the M.E. office and was told they would contact me when the bod...I mean Mom and Dad will be released. I requested they take their bodies to Crompy's. That's who took care of Grandma Jane when she died. We can see them once at the funeral home."

"Did the M.E. tell you when we'd learn anything?"

"Learn what, James?" I questioned.

"How they died, of course," he quipped.

"No. They didn't."

"I'd like their number, Amelia. I want to call and ask questions of my own."

I took out a small note pad, I had in my pocket. I had written down every phone call I'd made and every detail I'd been told. I handed the notebook to James for viewing. The Detective's card fell out and he picked it up for a quick glance. "I'm calling him, too," he said. He took his cell from his jacket pocket and began dialing.

"James, it's five in the morning. No one is going to give you any news at this hour," I irritatingly said. Still, he called the M.E.'s department first. On the fourth ring, I heard the muffled sound of a lady's voice say hello and something of an office greeting. James proceeded to tell her who he was and why he was calling. They exchanged a few sentences and then he hung up. I waited for him to volunteer what he discovered. "She can't give me any information over the phone. You are the only point of contact that she can talk to and that has to be in person. She suggested we wait until they call, once they have completed the autopsies," James shared.

There it was. The word I was avoiding. Autopsy. Perry's return to our table was a welcomed break in having to visualize my parents being examined. He handed me the letter which I turned over to James. "Where's the other two?" he asked.

"They don't belong to us, James.I already sealed the envelops and put the one addressed to this *Carol* person in the outgoing hotel mail. I'll give Uncle Michael's his, when he arrives."

James read the note, looked up at me wide-eyed and said, "Dad had an affair. Carol Ferguson is the woman."

———————

"That's ridiculous, James. Dad *did not* have an affair! Good grief, what's wrong with you?" I said in an elevated voice.

"Look," he continued, "I know you aren't going to like this, but it's the truth. Remember when Jasmin and I spent that weekend at the house to help Dad repair the roof? — it was after that big ice storm", he paused for my acknowledgment. "Well, Jasmin and I were staying in my old room…since converted into a study… and I found a picture of Dad and another woman in an old book. It was odd, but I assumed it was just one of the workers at the Center."

"Yes…?" I prodded.

"But then, I surprised Dad that Monday morning at the Center. Jasmin and I were heading back home to Seattle, but Dad had left the house early, so we hadn't said our goodbyes. The Center wasn't quite open yet, but the side door was unlocked and I went in. When I entered the back office, Dad, and this woman I'd seen in the photo, were in a full embrace and kissing. Shocked, but also indigent, I stood there staring at Dad."

James went on to explain that Dad escorted him out of the office and firmly suggested that he not say anything to Mom. He said it was a one-time error in his judgment and it wouldn't happen again. He made James promise to keep what he saw to himself. "I agreed but left telling him how disappointed I was in him."

I sat in my seat, unable to speak. These past two days were more than I could take. "Well, we will forget about it. There's no benefit in drudging this up now. We don't know that Carol Ferguson is that woman and I chose to believe it was just that one-time. Dad wouldn't have done that to Mom. So, let's just forget about this, ok?" I said in more of a statement than a question.

And so, funeral arrangements were made. We decided on a joint funeral rather than separate, although it begged the question of why they both die the same day.

In the end, we determined that everyone would know anyway, and there were so many out of town family and friends that it just made sense to have it together. The funerals would be Friday, November 12th.

On Thursday, all siblings, except Nathanial, were in town and staying at the Doubletree. Byron had flown in on Wednesday night, but decided that having a baby there was not wise so Parisa stayed home with Franki.

While it was good to see everyone, I had little reserve energy to fully appreciate that we were all in the same room together, at last. No one was able to locate Nathanial to let him know of this news, and that was a glaring omission to our family gathering. Nathanial and I had long since stopped being close, primarily because of his long absences — without calling or being reachable. Now, it had been a few years with no contact. I missed him.

Uncle Michael flew in from Southern California as did Mom's other brothers; Henry and Patrick, with their wives. It was a large crowd of family with a lot of black garments. The ceremony was at 2 p.m., at the chapel belonging to the funeral home. Dad had a Will that requested the chapel rather than the church he had once ministered. The five of us siblings had an appointment, with the family lawyer, for the following Monday to review the entire Will's contents. My sentimental- nature, seeing them in the caskets side by side, was tainted with the information James had given. I wanted to see it as somehow sweet that they left this world together, but all I could think was how they died and about this other woman. As hard as I tried, the image of Dad kissing someone, other than Mom, was gut-wrenching.

In traditional fashion, the ceremony honored them both with words of kindness and love. Stephen and Patrick gave the family eEulogy, and a few of Dad's past work-friends said a few words as well. From the Chapel, those that wanted could follow the caskets and family procession to the grave sites.

With more words spoken by the Cemetery Chaplain, the service concluded with a release of doves into the air. These two ceremonies might have been touching and meaningful to me, had it not been for the events leading to it. Instead, I felt numb and deeply hurt, and I hadn't even heard the whole of it yet.

We spent the weekend sleeping and meeting up for family, breakfasts at the hotel and lounging around together in our hotel suite. Perry had the sense to change our standard room to a full suite that included a small kitchen and living room area, knowing the family would need a place to be together. We seldom talked about how they died, assumingely too painful to have a round-table discussion. We brought in take-out food for lunches, but all retreated to our own rooms for evening respite and quiet processing. James and I were the only ones that knew of Dad's indiscretion, and it would stay that way until it was no longer possible.

11

The Will — Three & Four

Byron left on Sunday night to return to his family and to his business that needed attention. Mom's siblings and Dad's extended family, all flew out on Saturday, leaving just the O'Malley-Nolan children to stay and see the lawyer on Monday.

Monday, November 15th was a holiday for most, but not for Clement Waters, attorney at law. We all joined him in a conference room at 10 a.m. to hear how Dad and Mom wanted their assets distributed. We assumed that the house would be sold and split six ways, with little else of value to mention. Because of its expected simplicity, I was surprised that Clement wanted us all present. I was about to understand why.

Mr. Waters asked if we wanted him to read the entirety of the Will, or to just give us the high points. We all opted for the high points. James interjected that he would, also want to read the Will afterward. "Of course," was Clement's response.

The high points were as expected; the house went to the children and all of its contents to be divided equally. Dad said, in the Will, that he was confident we could all divide up the house belongings without a fuss. I was certain he was right. Mom's taste in furnishings, while always attractive, wouldn't likely be anything we would fight over.

What followed was less expected. Dad evidently had been saving, and had invested in the stock market. Between the two; savings and stock, there were nearly a million dollars. With this disclosed, we all looked at one another in disbelief and awe. "Dad did that?" Samuel said, while all of us were thinking the same thing. Dad was as thrifty as Mom, and we assumed every penny made, from both his preacher days, and that of the non-profit center, went into paying the bills and staying afloat. The news brought some quiet laughter and smiles to otherwise gloomy faces around that table. The laughter would be short-lived.

"I asked that you all be present not only for this surprising financial news, but for the last Will item," Clement said. "Your father has allocated $200,000, of his estate to Carol Ferguson and son, Kevin." The smiles disappeared and replaced with "What the fuck?" by Samuel. "Who's Carol Ferg…and who's Kevin?" he demanded.

James and I glanced at each other and knew our family was about to be cratered. James spoke up, "I don't know who Kevin is, but I know that Dad had an affair with Carol. Evidently, I didn't' know how serious it was." Under his breath, he added *Damn him.*

Now, all eyes were on Clement to explain anything further. "Kevin" he added in hesitation, "is your half-brother…your father's son with Carol. Kevin is 24".

"How old is Carol?", Samuel demanded. "I imagine she's a bit younger than your Dad," was Clément's politically correct response. In actuality, Carol was in her twenties when the affair started in 1977. Carol was now in her fifties — forty years Dad's junior. The relationship lasted for twenty years, only ending with Dad's onset of forgetfulness.

Here's the thing with knowing what you think you know. It's seldom right and 100% not really true.

———————

We all went home Tuesday, after the reading of the Will — each in our own heads, processing the contents and Dad's secret life. Samuel was still kicking furniture the last time I saw him at the hotel, and James kept an angry scowl on his face until we said goodby. The twins appeared to have compartmentalized it for the trip home, much like I had. I determined to put it aside and move on. Dad was not welcome in my head, and I was not going to let this turn me inside out, or at least that was the plan. I couldn't understand how he could have betrayed his family like that, but that was how it was.

Perry and I resumed our lives to its previous routines. I was researching material for my latest book, and Perry going off to work each morning. Our weekends were spent together with frequent trips to San Francisco, being grandparents to Franki. We liked to babysit at least once a month, so that Parisa and Byron could have a date night. Mom had given Perry and I this gift, when Byron was young, and we valued its byproducts. Perry and I remained in love, although it did appear less demonstrative than our younger days. Our sweet connection was more of quietness — unspoken words while holding hands in contentment.

Christmas and the New Year came and went with the usual celebrations. There was little mentioned of Mom and Dad that first year. I imagined we were still in shock. Although, I had taken some of the Christmas decorations out of their house, I didn't put them up.

On January 26th, Grandma Jane's birthday, I felt the need to go back to Fanny's diary and pick up where I had left off. The days of seeking answers to my dream-states, elicited by the release of my hair, seemed like someone else's life now. Still, out of the blue, I thought of the diary and impulsively began to read.

The last entry I had read, so long ago, was Fanny's marriage to Henry, the loss of a baby soon after, followed by the birth of Byron. Her entries were short with little information —

reading more like a list than a diary of thoughts and feeling. There were long gaps between entries; I supposed because of the business of birthing children and keeping house. I casually flipped through the pages of incidental entries;

March 3, 1882 Willian born. Named afta cousin . Ms O'Neil says hes a strappin' fella. Tired now.

By 1888, she would have five boys. I mused how different her life was to mine and how tired her body must have been, birthing a child nearly every year. There was no mention of Grandma Jane's birth in 1890, and in fact, there were no entries between 1886 and 1903. Then, an entry dated September 5, 1903, caught my eye as she writes that Henry has been ill and the loss of income troublesome. Then, *Februry 16, 1905 My Henry t'is det and t'is no longr sufferin. He t'is in heaven.*

Henry O'Malley, my Great Grandfather, died presumably of his illness. I did the math and found that Fanny was only 50 years old when she was widowed. Grandma Jane was 15, second to the youngest of the seven children and Byron the oldest at 24, and still living at home. I read an entry dated 1906, indicating they were no longer in Canada and the boys had started their own lumbering business. Ok, now I was hooked and needed to see how it all turned out. I returned to the 1906 entry and read on. Little was written, in this journal, of many details. Fanny did mention that both Jane and her sister Lucinda, were especially *frail* during the train trip out of Canada. An entry that bottomed my heart was this:

May 1906 Pleaze Lord, Byron, dont die. I wont be able to goes on, pleaze".

Byron died? On the train? This entry took me back to Mom's declared vision that Byron died on a train. As Dad had suggested, it was not *my* Byron, in Mom's premonition dream but that of her *Uncle* Byron, Fanny's son.

It was all I could read for now. Fanny, the same twelve-year-old girl that had joined me in the ocean waters, in an attempt to end her life, now endured the death of both her husband and her oldest child at the age of 51. What courage had it taken to pack up this family, leaving the only home they had ever known, and boarding a train to an unknown destiny. Then, during the trip, enduring the death of a child.

This entire story read like a suspense novel I might have picked up at a flea market, yet it was my own family's story. And while still not *my* life story, it penetrated my heart. My eyes welled up with tears. I had met Fanny. It was only in a mysterious and unexplainable time-warp, but I felt connected to her, and it was as if I was feeling some of her grief. "I'm so sorry Fanny," I said out loud. The Diary was put back in the storage box and returned to the shelf. With a big sigh, I wiped my tears and took a walk.

That Sunday, Perry and I drove to San Francisco to see Byron and the family. It was March 31st, and Franki was two years old. We were to have a big celebration. I welcomed the change in mood by seeing this sweet little girl play and laugh.

When we arrived, Parisa, her parents, and little Franki were busy readying the party atmosphere. "Byron's gone to pick up the cake" Parisa announced. "We love this little bakery in the Castro District but he shouldn't be much longer," she added.

Within five minutes of this announcement, the phone rang. Parisa answered and immediately handed it to me. "It's Byron," she said, returning to her business of blowing up balloons.

I took the phone and said a cheerful hello. "Mom. Uncle Nathanial is here. He's sitting in the café across the street. I barely recognized him, but it's him!" Byron said anxiously.

He knew that Nathanial's absence, over the past two years, was painful for me and that I often spoke of how I might find him. "Where are you? I'm coming to you. Don't lose him". I handed the phone to Perry, indicating that Byron was going to give him his location. I had never been good at directions and relied on Perry to get us to unknown destinations. Once off the phone, we briefly explained where we were going, and Perry and I walked briskly to the car.

Approaching the corner where Byron was standing, Perry let me off as he circled the block again in search of a parking place. As I approached Byron we hugged and then he immediately pointed to the café across the street. Sitting at a window table sat Nathanial, sipping from a coffee mug and perhaps writing in a journal. At first glance, all I noticed was how thin his face looked. His cheeks were sunken and hair disarray. I asked Byron to keep his dad company and then I crossed the street.

Entering the café, I slowly approached his table and took the seat across from him. As if he already knew who had sat down, he put the cup and pen down first, then looked up. "I wondered when this might happen," he said.

"Nathanial, we have all missed you so much. Why?" I asked. I was not prepared for his response but he gave it anyway. Nathanial had been in a love relationship. His name was Wayne. He had been happy, but hesitant to introduce Wayne to the family. With tears in his eyes, Nathanial told me that Wayne had died. I reached for his hand, but he pulled it back. "There's more," he quipped. "I'm dying. I have AIDS".

I didn't know what Nathanial expected from me with this news, but my response seemed to startle him.

"Nathanial, you are my brother. You know you're my favorite. You are my heart. There are advanced treatments now, and I want to help you. Your family needs you as much as you need us." I didn't tell him then, about Mom and Dad. That would be another day. We sat talking for another 30 minutes, and he finally agreed to return home with Perry and I.

He had no job and no healthcare insurance. He had not continued under a doctor's care, once diagnosed with AIDS, and his extreme weight loss was as much due to not eating as it was to the disease. We agreed to meet back at the café in a few hours, so that he could gather his belongings from a friend's home, where he had been living. Meanwhile, Perry and I returned to Byron's and celebrated Franki's second birthday. Nathanial didn't even know of Franki, so there was a lot of catching up to do.

As planned, we picked Nathanial up, on the corner near the café. He had one bag with him and a guitar. He looked even thinner standing there, jeans so baggy I was afraid they might fall off. We drove back across the Oakland bridge, and entered Nathanial into a well-known treatment program. He set up home in our guest room and day by day gained some weight and color back into his face. The prognosis, though, was not good. He had waited too long for care. Yet, the doctors were encouraged that Nathanial had some fight left in him, and whatever life he had left could be quality, under their care. We sat many mornings at the breakfast table, reminiscing and laughing at our childhood follies. I had my Nathanial back, and the world seemed right again.

I wondered how long it would take for him to ask, but I knew it was coming. Then, a morning in April, he did.

"So," he said, "have you called Mom and Dad yet, to tell them the prodigal son has returned?" There it was. I had dreaded this moment and now it was here.

"Nathanial, I have something to tell you, and it won't be easy to hear," I began.

I told Nathanial about Dad's diagnosis with Alzheimer's and moving them into a smaller home with nursing help. There was no easy way to tell the entire story, so I just took a breath and told him how they had died. I explained the day we learned about Dad's affair and that we had a half-brother…somewhere. As expected, Nathanial was in shock. In a 30 minute conversation, he had lost both his parents to a suicide and mercy killing, and learned of his father's secret life.

I didn't know if this revealing was the cause for his steady decline or just the poor prognosis, but within a month, Nathanial was hospitalized and placed in Hospice care. The medical goal was to keep him comfortable and manage his pain. I was there with him every day, and Perry would come after work.

Toward the end of May, we were allowed to bring him back to our home for his final days. A Hospice nurse came every other day to titrate his morphine and ease his breathing. I watched the slow death of Nathanial. By now, he was barely conscious and didn't speak. Periodically, he would open his eyes and give me a tender look telling me that, *It's ok, I'm ready.*

On May 28th, 2005, Nathanial Oliver O'Malley-Nolan died at 3 a.m. I had set up a cot in his room and was holding his hand, as he took his last breath. While ever grateful to have had Nathanial back in my life, I was even more honored to be with him during his death.

I'm not sure how the human heart survives such assaults. It does feel like it breaks, yet somehow continues to beat. Nathanial had requested no funeral and instead, *if you must do something* (said with his mischievous smile), *have a party with carrot cake and cream-cheese frosting, champagne and ragtime music.* That way, he said, he would still be there.

The cremated remains of Nathanial were scattered on the coast near Pacifica Beach, with a few of his San Francisco friends in attendance. The memorial party was held two weeks later, with all the food and music items requested. James, so far away in NYC, was with us via phone but otherwise, all of the Nolan clan; spouses and children, were present. Franki kept us from profound sadness with her silly dancing to the music and face covered in frosting. We toasted to Nathanial, and blessed his passing.

When all family had left, Perry and I sat in silence at the kitchen table with a cup of chamomile tea. As if he knew what I was thinking, he touched my hand and softly spoke. "It's not your fault, Amelia. You couldn't have kept the news from Nathanial. He had a right to know."

"I know," I said in reply, "but, I still wonder…if Mom hadn't taken their lives and we hadn't learned of Dad's other family, would Nathanial still be alive? It's just that I miss him so much."

"Of course, you do," was his only possible answer.

Nathanial's passing, and likely the accumulative of Mom and Dad's deaths, changed me. More accurately, the change began in small measures. I had quietly turned 50 while watching my soul-brother die. I didn't want a celebration or any fuss about entering my fifth decade. I somehow felt different, and I preferred to hide out.

My current research and book was more of the same; how our humanity is centered on tribal behavior and our need to belong even when it's caustic. I had made a name for myself in this academic arena and my publisher was urging me to complete the promised book. Instead, I would stare at the blank paper and feel nothing for its energy. I had stopped writing altogether.

On a warmer than usual September day, I shared with Perry my discontent and thoughts of writing about something else. As he always had been, he said something in the realm of; *I was a great writer, and anything I wrote would be great.*

But he also added that I might consider that I had already worked hard to build my audience, and changing now might negatively impact that. Of course, he was right, but I was also a bit disappointed that he didn't seem to connect with my changing heart. After thinking for a few days on that conversation, and all of the thoughts swirling in my head, I announced that I needed to get away — by myself — and sort this out.

"Where will you go?" Perry asked. I knew the answer in my heart even before I knew it in my head. "Minneapolis" I responded.

12

Final Act

I boarded a plane for Duluth. I had her address from Mom's pre-addressed envelope, and she agreed to meet with me. I was ready…no … needed to understand how or why Dad had left the vows of his marriage and his Christian faith. I needed to know this woman that my dad loved. I no longer felt the judgment of his behavior, nor did I wish to continue to ignore it. Perhaps I had learned a valuable lesson from my breakdown in 1992, at the conference.

The words of my comforting strangers; *One way or another grief will emerge. Sometimes it bubbles over, manifesting in illness, and other times in self-destructive behavior* — crept back into my consciousness and I didn't want a repeat performance.

I was ready to face my grief. Both Nathanial and Dad had deliberately chosen lives of secrecy. Could it be that Nathanial's hidden sexuality connected somehow to Dad's life of having a mistress? How is it the mind can live outwardly, what is complete torment inwardly?

Carol Ferguson opened her urban apartment door on the second knock. She stood 5 foot 5ish, about my age, slender, with short blonde hair. I immediately recognized that she looked nothing like Mom. Was this the attraction? She invited me in and guided us to her small, but stylish, living room. There were no thrift-store furnishings, and instead of a lingering musty-odor that often accompanied Mom's latest Good-Will find, Carol's home was fragrant with Lilac.

"Thank you for agreeing to meet with me. I'm sure this isn't easy…for either of us," I began.

She sighed and looked at her hands. Carol presented in blue jeans and a capped sleeve T-shirt. I acknowledged that she was a lovely looking woman. "What would you like to know?" she nervously asked. I explained what I already knew, and that I wanted to know about their relationship. Was it love? How did it happen? She began by telling me that it *was* love for them both. She also said that she wouldn't discuss the details of their relationship, but hoped that what she could offer would bring me peace.

"Your Dad and I worked together. I had come out of an abusive and harsh marriage just a year prior, and took the job at the Center because I knew what it was like to feel all alone and shunned by family. I don't know how any love begins, really," she added. "But, it did." She went on to reassure me that Dad loved Mom, and had told Carol he would never leave the marriage. It was a contention between them throughout the relationship.

"What did my dad tell you about his children? I mean, was he in conflict with having an affair…I mean, being with you?" I asked.

"Every day," was her response.

"Then I need to try to understand why he kept seeing you?"

Carol sat in silence for a few minutes before beginning to explain. "I don't know how much to tell you. I don't want to hurt you, Amelia."

"I've spent months thinking about this and, yes, at first I was angry and deeply hurt. Now, I'm ready to understand — well, to the extent a daughter can, so that I can heal. Can you help me do that, Carol?" It was the first time I had called her by name, and it somehow seemed to help us both make a connection.

"Your Dad was lonely. He loved your mother, but their relationship was platonic. It had been years since they had been intimate and he was lonely. At least that's how it began."

"Are you saying my Dad just wanted sex?"

"Stop! Amelia. I want to help you but I will not sit here and have you degrade your Father's life or the love we shared. If you want to hear this, I'll continue. If not, I'll call you a cab," she sternly quipped. I didn't want to mention I'd come in a rental car. That seemed petty to correct her, but now I was the one looking down at my hands.

"Ok, I apologize. This is harder than I thought. Please continue."

"All I know is that your dad didn't feel he had a full partner in his marriage. He said their conversations were limited to daily happenings and what the kids were doing. He wanted someone to share his feeling, but that was hard for your mom, or at least that was your Dad's perspective."

Yes, that was probably all true. Mom tried to avoid all unpleasantries. Her life was about keeping the home and boasting about our Irish roots.

"Your Dad bragged about all of you. He had a huge heart and many of our long talks were about you and your brothers. He was proud of each of you. Even when Nathanial came out, he talked about how much he loved him, and how he hoped Nathanial felt his love."

"Did Dad fear of being found out?" I asked carefully. By now I was not sure of the boundaries and what might send Carol reaching for the phone.

"Yes. All of the time. He was tormented and conflicted. Our secret lives were carefully guarded. You all were first in his life., though. But he wanted more — and I loved him — so I allowed for his prolonged absences. You had the best of him and we had what he could give." There it was. "We." It was my permission to step in that direction.

"Where is Kevin, now?" I asked.

"He works in town. He and his wife run an computer repair shop," she answered.

"Did Dad have a relationship with him?"

"Of course. He loved him. Would you like to meet him?" she questioned. I thought for a moment and answered, "No, not this time. This has been a lot to take in for now." I slowly rose and walked to the door. I took Carol's hand and thanked her.

I left for my rented cabin on Lake Superior. There, I hoped to process, think and write. I had received what I came for — minus the *understanding*. That would to come in the quietness of my seclusion.

Before settling into the cottage, I called Perry, and told him of the conversation. He was politely quiet through my 10 minute-recall of all the details and the interjection of what I had felt with each disclosure. I paused, and he only said, "that's a lot of information." I went on to speak about my feelings, that I was conflicted. I wanted to like Carol and meet my half- brother but also felt it might somehow betray Mom. "Talk to me, Perry," I said when there was more silence on the other end.

"I'm here to support you, honey. You will figure it out." Now, I was the one silent. My mind immediately went to Mom and her reluctance to discuss anything about feelings or negative subjects.

"Fiddle-dee-dee, Let's make tea!" she would say to change a subject that was uncomfortable. Was Perry unable to have this discussion? I realized that we both had been avoiders and our conversations never amounted to much more than the news of the day, the weather or plans for the weekend. Even when Mom and Dad died, we avoided talking about it, replacing it with tender hand holding, hugs, and comforting food. But now something had shifted in me. Avoidance and small talk were not enough.

As I hung up the phone the words of Lord Byron pierced my heart:

Oh, talk not to me of a name great in story;
The days of our youth are the days of our glory

I had entered into a new frontier. I was being unearthed. And I was alone.

While Perry didn't understand, I needed to extend my time in the Minnesota cabin. My head filled with insights I hadn't considered before, and my writing was flowing. Nightly check-ins with Perry were becoming increasingly frustrating, for both of us.

"I don't understand, Amelia. You've been gone a week now, and you want to stay longer? What's going on?" he asked.

"Perry, I need this. I'm coming to terms with all that I've lost and for the first time in my life, finding who I really am!"

"Can't you do that here — at home?" he added.

Each night, a version of this conversation ensued. It was true, I was upsetting our cart. We had never been apart for more than one night in our 29-year marriage. Perry had been my world and my rock, in which to gauge my existence. I imagined it must have felt scary for him, to be losing that.

I tried to reassure him that this was time for me, rather than time to be away from him. The truth was, it was both. Like Mom, my self-worth tied around our marriage. I was an accomplished writer and author and known in my circle of academia with a small circumference of respect. In my social world, I had not considered myself as separate from Perry, because all of my decisions centered around the norm of my marriage. Being normal was not a bad thing, but it was occurring to me that it was an incomplete-thing. I had not been brave.

The time away was helping me sort through this well-learned attribute of being a *pleaser*. I was not in the blaming-game, although I realized that I had learned this from watching Mom. Conflict in my childhood home, was not permitted and squelched at every level. Being moral and Irish was all that mattered. I understood that it was probably what Mom had learned in her childhood, and she had never re-considered it for its usefulness. I also realized the discontent Dad must have felt. He wanted complete intimacy with his wife; emotional, intellectual and physical — but was lacking two of the three, perhaps all three.

But there was something else. Underneath all of this reconciling of my youth, the secrets revealed and deaths of those I loved; I knew that the visitations with my great grandmother, had significance. I had a soulful intuition that the family "gift" had been trivialized as just a unique thing we shared. Even I had tucked away my experiences, and packaged them in a neat little mind-box to take off the shelf at my whim. I somehow knew there was something more profound to these cross overs.

The thought both frightened me and excited me. I was a psychologist in the area of brain science. What I was now thinking about was more in the category of paranormal science. While I had no ambitions to frontier new ground in this area; I needed to look at it for myself.

There's a philosophy out of Sweden that's called InnSaei. It means *The Sea Within* or in psychology, *To See from the Inside Out*. It's about a *knowing* that's beyond our five senses. I was *knowing*, now, that these cross overs were there as part of my unearthing. Mom had not wanted to know, and Grandma Jane was lost in its fanciful notion. I wanted more, and I instinctively knew there *was* more. What I didn't know was how to approach it. I had been as guilty to box it away.   This circled back to my realization that I was more like my Mom than I wanted to admit.

In my second week, at the cabin, I was beginning to make a different choice for myself. How it would manifest, I still didn't understand. I did know that I had unfinished business here in Minnesota, so I made the call.

"Hi Carol, this is Amelia again," I said into her phone machine. "I'd like to meet Kevin. I'm still in the area, and can meet at his convenience. Please call me." It was less than an hour later than Carol called back and we set up a meeting time in downtown Duluth, at a Starbuck's. Kevin wanted to meet me, too, Carol said.

Kevin was 25 years old, and I was 51. He was my brother and I knew nearly nothing about his life. I had not even seen a picture of him. The need to meet him was based purely on the decision to be brave .I didn't want to continue the pattern of hiding behind what I was afraid of, or didn't not understand. If I was going to make a different path for my life, it began here.

As I pulled up to the coffee shop, I felt butterflies leaping inside my gut. It was not dread. — it was excitement. I entered through a side door and immediately spotted Kevin. It took my breath. He looked so much like Nathanial that my mind needed to readjust and regain presence. James and Nathanial were spittin' images of Dad while the twins, Jack and Samuel favored Mom's side. I walked over and held out my hand in an introduction. We sat in awkwardness for a few moments, but I couldn't help but warm to him with his family resemblance and warm demeanor. Kevin was funny, witty and genuine.

I had brought pictures of Byron, Parisa, and Franki, and asked if he wanted to see them. "I'm an Uncle!" he said, gazing closer at Franki's picture. "Yes, you are," I smiled. We exchanged phone numbers and addresses, with the mutual invitations to stay in touch.

As I was leaving, Kevin touched my arm and said: "Amelia, I've been an only child until today." We hugged affectionately, and I departed with a sense of completion. Kevin could have chosen a path of resentment, that his father was not available for much of his childhood, but he didn't. The judgment and fear that could have so easily remained locked inside, were wiped away with truth and reality — for both of us.

Returning to my retreat on the lake, I wrote down these thoughts and questions that were popping up: What's the purpose of the cross over experiences? What is the relationship between Fanny and I? What has happened now, to make me start caring?

The answers to these questions, and a hundred more, would not be answered that night. With that, I turned off the light and went to bed.

I had, thoughtlessly, gone to bed without calling Perry. I dialed him up before my first cup of coffee the next morning. The phone rang without him answering, and eventually it went to voicemail. I left him an apology for not calling sooner, and a brief synopsis of my time with Kevin. I had accepted the fact that my new found *need to talk over my feelings* had not produced the warm-fuzzies with Perry. While I longed for him to ask all the right questions, and even give his perspective, I was no longer expecting it. I loved Perry, and it would all somehow work out.

Much of that day was spent either working on a new project, a clear departure from my normal scholarly work, or taking another cup of coffee out to the deck and reveling in the fall foliage and still waters. This lake-gazing was a dramatic shift from my once busying-self.

I welcomed this solitude and stillness. At 4 p.m., Perry called. He gave a matter of fact report of his day's errands, not acknowledging my message about meeting my secret brother. This awkwardness between us was new territory. When it was my turn to talk, I, too, listed my day's activities, rather than telling him all the feelings going on inside.

"I woke up around seven after going to bed early. I wrote until noon and then took a break, returning to my writing until your call," was all I offered. Perry didn't ask me when I might be coming home and I didn't offer, although I felt my time there coming to a logical end. We hung up the phone with our customary "love you's", and I returned to the deck and my thoughts.

On Tuesday, I boarded a plane for home. I had been gone for nearly two weeks and knew that my re-entry might be clumsy for both Perry and I. On my way from the airport, I picked up two steaks and salad fixings. Arriving home before Perry's return from work I prepared dinner and set the table with candlelight and cloth napkins. It was a white-flag offering, because I was certain Perry had taken my time away as a personal affront on him.

His arrival was on time, and he noticed the effort I put into our dinner. Our conversation was primarily about what silly thing Franki had done during my absence, or a report of the antics at Perry's office.

That night, we made love as if I had never left, and as if I were the same person I was when I had left. At the end of our intimacy, Perry thanked me. I was not sure how to take that. Was he thanking me for sex or for coming home? Without asking, I quietly said goodnight and rolled over.

Marriage is not a difficult relationship when both people are on the same page emotional and intellectually. When they are, life is amenable. When there's a change in one or both, and the planes tilt, and it can become the hardest relationship imaginable.

––––––––

Thanksgiving was at Byron and Parisa's with Samuel, Uncle Michael, Aunt Vanessa and a few of Byron's colleagues from his business, in attendance. Perry and I had settled back into our daily and weekend routines and on the outside it seemed my September hiatus left us without a mark. Inside however, I knew I was different and had not yet figured out how to interact with Perry while remaining true to myself.

After the family dinner, Byron and I slipped away to the backyard patio, for some time alone. Byron and I had talked two weeks after my return from Minnesota. I had shared with him how my life was changing, and I didn't know how to *be* that change. As we now sat and held our overly full bellies, Byron offered up his thoughts.

"Mom, Dad seems a little down lately. I'm wondering… and I know it's none of my business….but are things ok with you two?" It had never occurred to me that anyone on the outside could see our internal struggles.

"We've fine, Byron. Every couple goes through bumps, but we love each other, and we'll figure this out," I said reassuringly. I did believe this, but I also knew that Perry didn't seem his old self since my return.

When I did ask him if he wanted to talk or if anything was wrong, he would laugh it off and say, "There's nothing to talk about, Amelia. You think too much!"

"I need to find my own outlet for this *new-me* thing that's going on," I continued explaining to Byron. "I have connected with a woman's group, through the University, which meets and talks about loss and menopause. Sounds weird, right?" I added. Byron smiled and nodded in approval.

"Still, I think I'll talk to Dad," he said. "Maybe it's a guy-thing, and I can help."

Just before leaving the festivities, Byron glanced my way and gave me a thumbs-up and broad smile. I knew that Perry would have told his son that everything was fine, regardless of what might be going on. I also understood that Perry might not even be aware of what he was feeling. I made a decision, standing in Byron's foyer, to make this marriage right again. I loved this man, and I wanted him to feel that love. Whatever self-discovering was going on within me, I was still his life-partner, and he was still my dearest and oldest friend.

On our drive home, I reached over and held his hand tenderly. "Perry, you are still the love of my life. I know my time away changed things, but it didn't change my love for you."

It was as if a weight lifted off of his shoulders, and I watched his posture change from slouch to sitting tall. He closed his eyes for two seconds, sighed deeply and squeezed my hand. I knew, then, that he had been afraid that I would leave him.

"We're good," he said, and then the conversation turned to the funny things Franki had done at the dinner table with the turkey bone. It was good to laugh with Perry, and our love grew in that car, on that night.

Christmas would be at our place that year. Franki was approaching three and still more interested in the twinkly lights and the wrapped boxes than having an understanding of Santa Claus and receiving gifts. Byron and Parisa had a party to go to in Los Angeles ,so Franki was to spend a few days and nights with Nana and Dat. I had chosen my grandparent name, *Nana*, but Franki had come up with the name *Dat* to call Perry.

She was a joy and a bundle of constant energy. Both Perry and I were exhausted when she finally went to bed at 8 p.m. "This is why children are only given to women with Estrogen!" I mused. Even though I had overdone it running and chasing her throughout the house, in a game of hide-n-seek, Perry looked the worse for the wear.

Byron was to be back for her in the morning, and while we loved her with all our hearts, we were looking forward to the bulk of that next day doing nothing! After picking up the toys and finishing the dinner dishes, Perry and I went to bed at 9:30.

"It was a good day," Perry said. "I love you, Amelia." Perry rarely said the words unless it was the usual goodbye quip on the phone.

"I love you, too, Dat," I returned. I turned out the light and heard his gentle snoring within five minutes, and it made me smile.

I woke first, even before Franki. Slipping out of bed careful not to wake Perry, I started the coffee and quietly began to make the batter for *Franki-pancakes*. She could eat a half dozen of these letter pancakes. I would start with the letter F, for her name, and as long as she was still wanting, I proceeded down the letters. In just 20 minutes, Franki was awake and calling out for me to help her potty. With her PJs still on, she climbed up the kitchen chair and positioned herself for pancakes. "Mor, mor, Nana" she would say.

Byron arrived an hour later, and Franki greeted him with open arms and a hug around his neck. I never tired of seeing my precious son engulfed in the tiny arms of his own child.

"Dad up?" Byron asked. "I wanted to tell him about fishing rod I saw in LA."

"Come to think of it; he's sure sleeping in. I think our little girl wore him out! Go in there and see if his awake," I encouraged. Byron headed to the master bedroom while Franki and I returned to the kitchen table for her breakfast dessert of blueberries. She liked them frozen, not thawed, and every time she would remind me and say "Foz'n, Nana. Not fawed, member?"

With blueberries in place, I refilled my coffee, and when I turned back around, Byron was standing in the hallway just staring at me, his face drained of color.

"Byron, are you ok?" I asked, but in one second I knew it was Perry that was *not* ok. I ran toward him trying to get to the bedroom.

"Mom, he's gone. He's been gone for a while," he said softly.

"NO" I shouted, call an ambulance! Byron!" Byron held me tight, and I melted onto the floor. He sat there with me until Franki came over to us. She began to cry and Byron helped me up. He picked up Franki and we all went over to the living room sofa. Byron made a few calls one of which was to Parisa, asking her to come pick up Franki.

The next few hours were a fog. I remembered the stretcher coming in, and Perry going out. I asked to see him, but the funeral worker said it was best that I wait. Later, in my right mind, I understood that Perry had probably died shortly after going to sleep. His body cold and malformed in death, wouldn't have been a good last vision of him.

We would later learn that Perry had suffered a major heart attack and more than likely, didn't suffer. His primary physician thought it was a clotting defect, and nothing could have prevented it.

Byron stayed at the house for three days. He was trying to be strong, but his father's death had aged him considerably. To deal with his pain, Byron argued with the physician; "How could you NOT know!" he shouted into the phone referring to Perry's clotting disorder.

For Byron, Perry's death needed to make sense. His father was only 52 and by all appearances, healthy. I knew I couldn't help Byron resolve this. It was his path and his journey. Instead, I would merely hug him, or start a conversation reminiscing about Perry and the good father that he was.

"Byron, have I ever told you about the day your Dad proposed to me?" I asked. Byron seemed intrigued, so I told him the story of the lake, getting on one knee, the ring and then I told him about letting down my hair and the vision of the Blayney children dancing.

"You've never told me this story, Mom. What was that like for you, seeing the children dancing that weren't really there? It was freaky when it happened to me!" he offered.

"Well, I don't know. I didn't think of it as scary or anything. Later, looking at the family photos, I could identify all but a few of the children I saw. Grandma Fanny and her siblings were all there."

At that, Byron said, "I miss him so much, Mom."

"I know, son. I miss him too. He was too young to leave us." We held each other, and for the first time in three days Byron cried.

The funeral was on a Wednesday. Neither Perry nor I attended any church, but we had long admired a small country-looking chapel on the outskirts of town. Perry's Advanced Directive declared his wish to be cremated, with no further instructions on what to do with the ashes. Before his cremation, however, I took it upon myself to have him in a closed casket for our goodbyes. There was standing room only in the small chapel. All of the Nolan children and their families came as did Mom's aging sibling's.

Perry's family was from Nebraska, and his parents had moved back there shortly after our wedding. His father had died the year before Grandma Jane. His mother came to the funeral and brought a cousin with her that no one had ever heard of before. Perry was not close to his family, and I had often wondered why, but he had never volunteer information about his childhood, and I never asked. He had always said that he loved just being a part of the O'Malley Nolan clan and "that's enough."

Perry hated black clothing so I wore a lavender silk suit with a pale yellow magnolia flower on the lapel. While it was surreal to be at my husband's funeral, I felt the strength in me that I had not felt at Mom and Dad's funeral or Nathanial's memorial. Was I numb to all the deaths that happened in a short span of time or was this a piece of my inner transforming? I tried not to evaluate it. Instead, I absorbed the love that filled the room in honor of a man I had loved all of my adult life.

The church-ladies organized a potluck of sandwiches and cake set up in the church basement. We had not asked for this, but they offered, and we accepted. At the day's end, the immediate family came back to the condo for coffee and comforting. It was a long day, but I was so pleased with the number of people that came, and I was proud for my husband.

The strength I felt that first week after Perry's death was fueled by the outpouring of love from others. Once the visitations and condolence cards slowed, the stark reality of my loss engulfed me. The nights were the worse — the despair tangible. Sometimes I couldn't stand to be in the condo. This is when I began my late night running. I ran to *not* feel. I ran in hopes of forgetting, if only for an hour, what I had lost. Eventually, I didn't need to go out into the night. Instead, I began to write. I wrote about Fanny and every event that had led up to that hour. I was reconciling a life destined to be alone.

The Holidays went by and if it hadn't been for Franki, I am confident we would have avoided the celebration entirely. Even as the New Year arrived and for weeks later, my grieving continued in waves. Somedays I was strong, feeling that Perry was still lingering which made me feel melancholy but content. Other days, I would write, weep and worry. My income wouldn't sustain the cost of my living expenses and Perry's life insurance policy was the standard issued with employment. A significant portion of that went toward his funeral and cremation and the other to pay off his car. What was left would take me through six months of staying at the condo — if I were frugal.

Since Perry was our financial guru, I wasn't even sure what being *frugal* might entail. It was in these moments that I grieved heaviest. I wasn't only mourning for the absence of Perry, but for the life I had so carefully set up. I was grieving for my loss of an interdependent self. I had depended on Perry for my financial security and now I was clueless. I didn't know how to pay off the car — Byron did it for me which reinforced how inept I was to manage my affairs. I didn't know the terms of the insurance policy, the mortgage details or even the balance in our joint bank account. Fortunate for me, others did know and helped just when needed. Life would change for me, and I was scared.

The doorbell rang just as I was ending one of my poor-Amelia weeping marathons. It was Fed Ex with a large envelope. My stomach came into my throat. Was this an eviction notice? Since I didn't know anything about how a mortgage worked, I was not sure!

Maybe a letter from Perry's secret lover?

Now, you're just being ridiculous, Amelia, I scolded. Whatever it was, it's *not* that but it can't be good either.

Instead of opening it, I carried it inside, sat on the floor and took down my hair.

Rising to the Top

He who knows others is wise; he who knows himself is enlightened.

~Lao Tzu

13

Being Brave

Before the last hairpin was released, I prayed. I didn't know if I was praying to God or to Fanny. I needed something more from Fanny, — than just being a bystander. Was that possible? I was a strong woman, but I was tired and needed help.

"Give me answers. Give me wisdom," I prayed. My hair cascaded down in front of my face, as my head bowed against my bent knees. I began to quietly cry for my loss, while a host of images floated past as if a slide show; my childhood, pregnant with Byron, wedding day, Nathanial, Mom, Dad…Perry. My mind floated further, and I found myself standing in a wooded area, with partially grey skies over head, and a lake in the distance.

Then I saw them. Two women were sitting on a large log, talking. They dressed in period clothing, and both appeared to be about my age. I walked closer to hear their conversation. I was certain that the woman in the green frock was Fanny.

"You can't just leave, Fanny. All of your bairns, 'tis here!" said the other woman. "You will starve your children. Stay here, and we will all help."

Fanny was looking at her lap, as the other woman spoke, and then it was her turn. Fanny spoke in a slight Irish accent, one I hadn't noticed when she spoke underwater all those years ago.

"Henry wanted this for the boys. There's nothin' here for them but there's hope in the evergreens. I have to give them a chance. Lucy and Jane need husbands and I don't want them going away from me to find them. I'm going no matter, dear sister."

They sat in silence for a few moments and Fanny continued. "'Tis not just for the children that we'll go. 'Tis for me, too. I want more than Riceville cares to offer. I want more, Amelia."

"Fanny, this is nonsense. You can't go. The train ride will kill you all, and you don't know what's beyond. Please stay with your family," her sister pleaded. Then the scene shifted as Fanny turned toward me, as if she had suddenly sensed my presence. My heart froze as she looked straight at me.

"Amelia," she said. The other woman replied, "Yes?" but I knew she was not addressing her sister.

"Amelia, you must go, too. It's time for you to blossom and rise to the top. It's time for you to be brave."

"Go where?" I asked her.

"You will know," was her only reply. The other woman didn't answer her, and it occurred to me that perhaps, like the time in the water, Fanny was speaking to me in thought, and I was hearing her.

"Fanny, do you know who I am?" I asked even though she had since turned back around. Turning again to face me she said,

"You are the one that saved me. You are my kin, my blood and we journey together," was her quiet reply.

Then the two women stood, and walked a dirt path that led into the woods. I knew I was not to follow.

Returning to the floor in my living room, where I sat, I gathered my hair and fastened it back up.

Amelia, you must go, too. It's time for you to blossom and rise to the top.

I was sure she was talking specifically to me. I was not merely an observer of a past scene. I was there, and she saw me! My great grandmother spoke and interacted with me — she knew me. What did she mean that I saved her? Was this a metaphor for something specific? Now, analyzing this, I wished I had stayed longer … followed them or asked more questions. It also occurred to me that I had received just what I had prayed for. I had asked for help and wisdom. Somewhere in what Fanny said, I would find it.

Be brave, she said. I had already been pondering this for my life, but had put it on a shelf once I had returned from Minnesota. Being brave was already something I had been questioning for myself.

With renewed strength, I opened the envelope, bracing myself for another trial by fire. Inside was a letter from Perry's life insurance company. *We are sorry for your loss*, it read. *Your claim is settled*, in bold print.

Most of the insurance money was already allocated, the funeral paid for with my credit card and the car paid off with savings. Now, I wished I hadn't spent my savings.

I reached inside the envelope for the check, and admonishing myself to deposit it that day and pay off the credit card. This whole financial world I had so carefully avoided with Perry, was unnerving me. Be brave, Amelia.

I held the check in my hands and stared, trying to comprehend the numbers. $1,000,000. Perry's life insurance was only $25,000! I knew this because he had kept his financial papers in a folder in our office. Byron had found them, and we had planned around those documents. I picked the letter back up, and read the last paragraph that offered more condolences and a phone number should I need anything further. Still searching for answers, I saw the letter's date printed in the top right-hand corner along wit:

Beneficiaries:

Amelia O'Malley Nolan $750,000

Byron O'Malley Nolan $250,000.

Getting myself off the floor, I went for the phone and dialed the provided number. The insurance company's claims representative confirmed the amount. Perry had added the additional premium a year ago, and designated the amounts to his wife and his son. As I hung up the phone, a teardrop fell on the receiver, and a smile replaced the frown.

Of course, I said to myself. *Perry would take care of his family.*

For the next six months, my heart stirred and turned over many times in planning for what was next for my life. Byron and Parisa announced that they had decided to move to L.A. by the end of the year, to be closer to Parisa's growing work and access to the fashion industry. The inheritance money, from his father, would allow Byron to make this move and invest more in the business.

"Mom, we want you to come with us to L.A.. Sell the condo and come live near us. We might even find a place where we both could live. Franki would love that." It had never occurred to me to sell the condo and to move. Byron opened a door that would end up changing my life in significant ways.

I was now 52 years old and could do about anything. There was no job to hold me, and I could write anywhere. The money Perry had left was enough to support me for a long time, especially if I were careful with my spending. As the summer waned, I had a plethora of ideas and options weighing in. By September, nearly nine months after Perry's death, I knew what it was I wanted to do. Calling Byron, I asked if I could come over and talk.

Nervous but excited as well, I drove to their apartment without help. Perry's death had caused many changes, and one of them was my determination to drive in the city without fear. My arrival was greeted with the usual warm hugs and Franki precious greeting as she ran into my arms. "Nana!" Her enthusiasm, to see me, lifted my spirits, but also gave me pause to what I was about to disclose. Parisa made coffee, and we sat down around the kitchen table. Franki busied herself with playdoe, on the kitchen floor, while the adults chattered.

"I've made a decision on what I'm going to do," I said. There was silence, as an invitation for me to continue. "I'm going to travel and write. I'm going to keep the condo and rent it out — for at least a year, I'm going to travel beginning in Belize and take it from there." From the look on their faces, I was certain that this idea had never occurred to them. I worried if they would try to talk me out of it, like Fanny's sister had tried with her. I added, "I won't be gone the entire time. I'll fly back into L.A. regularly to see you, and keep my relationship with Franki. That's important to me." Then I waited for their reaction.

"Mom, I'm so surprised. I didn't know you would even consider this. But I think it's great! I think you're brave!" Byron said. Parisa nodded and smiled broadly.

"Whew," I said. "I was a bit worried you'd think I was either crazy or reacting too soon after your dad's death." We continued to talk it over, and there was nothing but praise and encouragement. I think for both of us, we needed the permission to move forward, toward our dreams and a life without Perry.

It was unspoken, but we all felt our moves did not diminish our love for Perry or that we had forgotten him. I was also certain that this decision, to travel, wouldn't be as easy, or as romantic, as it sounded. In fact, I was counting on it challenging me, and to propel me forward in the transformation that had begun over a year ago.

Fanny had taken her family of seven, on a train West, with no real idea of what they would find upon arrival. But she knew that staying in the *old* was not an option. She was brave, much braver than I. I had books and the internet to pave my path. I had safety nets financially. The only thing I could claim as brave, was that I was doing this alone. There were no parents or husband to make the decisions. It was all on me and, frankly, I was petrified. Still, I wouldn't allow my fear to stop what I felt deep inside was necessary.

Three months later, on January 2nd, 2007, I boarded the plane to Belize City, Belize. My condo was rented out to a lovely couple; I had sold the cars and put my personal belongings in a 10x5 storage unit. I had one suitcase on wheels and a small backpack. This was my life for the next year.

Fanny, I'm on my way to the top!

————————

I landed in Belize City, knowing no one, and having never been anywhere other than Washington to California — let alone out of the country. With travel guidebooks in hand, I clumsily maneuvered my travel arrangements from the airport east to San

Ignacio, in the Caye's District of Belize. I had a reservation, for a month, at a studio apartment in the downtown area. This reservation turned into three months.

My life consisted of coffee in the café below the apartment in the morning and, writing in the afternoon until 3ish. I'd often walk near the river for a few hours, where I sometimes cried for Perry, or sat on the banks and just marveled at how my life had changed. The Maya ruins, nearby, were my favorite day-off adventure. The people in this small village were friendly, and I was continually asked to join them at café tables or park benches. They were genuine and kind.

My apartment, on Burn's Avenue, was sparsely furnished with marginal plumbing. I could have stayed at a more modern hotel, but I wanted to enjoy the culture and be in the mix of real-life. Earlier that year, there had been an archeological dig on Burn's Avenue, where Maya ruins were discovered. I wouldn't have found that at a Marriott.

Metaphorically, I imagined that I was the ruins being dug up. I was here being unearthed, one brush stroke at a time. My head and eyes had already been exposed, and I could see a whole new world before me. While I treasured my pre-existence, as Perry's wife, this was now the life I was choosing to live.

I met Clare one day at the café below my flat. She was also an American and here for healing. She had left her husband, of many years, and in the process of deciding whether to end it in divorce. Our stories were very different, in what brought us here, but the unearthing process was very similar. Like me, Clare had lived a sheltered and protected life as a married woman. One day, after many episodes of unkindness at the hands of her husband, Clare was finished pretending it would change. She packed a bag, fixed his dinner one last time, and ended up on an airplane. She told me she had been willing to let go of every single possession, in her big beautiful house, to find peace and joy. Clare left San Ignacio, for parts unknown. I never saw her again and have often wondered what became of her. The conversations with Clare made me wonder how many woman go through this unearthing, or feel the anxiousness of a life *less-lived*.

Was this the *rising to the top* that Fanny spoke?

My writing, while in San Ignacio, had been generically about me and these self-discoveries. At some point, however, I turned my attention toward a broader picture. I wanted to know if women, *of a certain age*, are drawn toward wanting more. With children grown or careers established, women in their 50's seek a higher purpose. With the waning of estrogen, (used to nurture the young and add peace to the home) the research suggests that women begin experiencing a different drive.

I wanted to talk and write about this type of personal transformation. It wasn't scholarly, and my publisher declined to entertain my submissions, calling my departure from my academic writings, *a crying shame*.

For me, the shame would be to continue on a path that was not mine to travel anymore. Blessed with the capability to see where these new writings might go, I could do nothing but forge ahead.

From San Ignacio, I flew back into L.A., for a visit and Franki's fourth birthday celebration. Byron and family had just moved and settled in a small home on the outskirts of Orange County. I slept on a hide-a-bed sofa, in their living room. Having just spent three months on a mattress, of questionable material, in Belize, this bed was the Hilton.

At first, I was glad to be back in the world of fabulous plumbing. But as my three-week family-hiatus was nearly the end, I longed to be back on the road.

In early Spring, I caught a plan to Leon, Mexico. Clare had told me about a town north of Mexico City, where she'd begun her travels. It was an *artist's town*, Clare called it, but she longed for more solitude and quiet, which had led her to move on to Belize.

An artist's town seemed perfect to me. I was a full-time writer now. I wanted — no needed, kindred spirits and help to navigate my new world. Taking a bus out of Leon, I arrived in San Miguel de Allende at 3 p.m. Clare had given me the name and email address of the woman her friend, Frank, rented from. I had made a reservation for another studio apartment in town. I had also learned, from Clare, a few things about taxi fare and pesos.

I hailed a taxi outside of the bus station and gave him my destination. The drive was 10 minutes, most of which was over uneven cobblestone roads. As the taxi driver pulled up to the historically looking building that would serve as my new home, I handed him 50 pesos. He wished me well and welcomed me to San Miguel.

My flat was a few degrees more modern than San Ignacio, but the structure inside and out was old. Still, for only 450 US dollars a month, I was thrilled to be near the town center, café's, old churches and the people. The first night, I met a couple from Australia.

Bart and Bruce had been on the road for two years, and both were artists. We hit it off right away, and there was a sense of being with Nathanial when Bruce and I spoke. He was clever and funny. He wrote articles for *Being Me*, a gay community online newsletter about traveling. Bart was a painter and had sold some of his work, in the town center, during a local art show. Between the two of them, their income was less than $15,000 a year yet, they seemed always to find the best lodgings or housesitting gigs. From Bart and Bruce, I learned about the joy of doing with little.

My time in San Miguel was magical. I seldom wrote in my flat. Instead, I took my computer, or sometimes a notepad and pen, into Centre and sat at a café to write. Everything was so inexpensive that I allowed myself to eat out once a day, spending hours in town, with the action of the city as my background music.

High tourist season was ending, so the crowds thinned a bit. The afternoon summer rains were heavy and often accompanied by thunder and lightning, which only added to the charm. I met Naomi, on such a day, in a running-retreat from a downpour. We nearly collided with each other, dashing into an open café. Making our simultaneous apologies, we laughed and sat down together ordering, *douc café, gracious*. As had so often happened in my travels, the right person showed up at just the right time. I had nearly completed a book and had no idea who or how to publish.

Naomi was a 45-year-old independent publisher and editor. She had left her high-profile position at a major publishing house, to *discover* herself. Naomi was fluent in Spanish, which I envied, and had set up her own business in San Miguel. Over three coffees, she educated me on how to get my manuscript read. She would take it on herself, but she specialized in children's books and illustrators.

Naomi gave me the name and contact information for three possible publishers. Synchronicities. I had gone from academics to serendipitous encounters. With her permission, I added Naomi's escape to my collection of *women-of-a-certain-age* transformation stories.

Except for two visits back to the states, in August and at Christmas, my time in San Miguel de Allende was my home for the rest of that year. On December 12th, the second year anniversary of Perry's death, I took a fluted glass, filled with champaign, out to my apartment balcony and toasted him. He probably wouldn't recognize the woman I'd blossomed into, but I think he would have approved. Every day I thought of Perry but rarely cried anymore. I could see the progress and hoped for a day when thinking of him didn't sting anymore.

That day almost came when Dawes walked into the room.

14

Dawes

The New Year came in with clear blue skies and crisp morning air. I was sitting at my usual bistro on the corner near the Jardin. Usually, I sat outside, but today I opted to use my computer to write. I chose a corner table, just inside the cafe door out of the bright sunlight. I was deep in thought, oblivious to what was around me, when he spoke.

Dawes' statue couldn't be ignored, standing over six-feet tall and sporting broad shoulders. His wavy hair and Marlboro-man whiskers made him stand out in the Hispanic environment. "You look deep in thought. A message from your lover?" he said in his yet unidentified accent.

I looked up, a bit annoyed at the interruption, and said, "What?"

"It's just that you must be writing a passionate love letter to be in such concentration!" he replied immediately.

"Do I know you?" I asked, still annoyed.

"That depends on your answer." Without an invitation, he sat in the chair across from me. I was speechless as I often became when confronted with strong personalities.

"Well?" he prodded.

"Well, what?" I said now mellowing against his striking handsomeness.

"Are you writing to your boyfriend, planning your next randevu?"

Smiling now, "No, I'm writing…my book."

"Then no we don't know each other but let's change that. I like the way you look," he kidded with a smirk.

Dawes was a southern boy from Tennessee, looking for anything other than conventional. What I assumed would be a shallow, but amusing, conversation with a handsome man, turned out to be filled with self-disclosures and thoughtful conclusions.

Dawes asked me questions about my book, life in California, and even about Perry's death. Dawes didn't dismiss my serious nature or try to change the subject. He listened and responded like no conversation I had ever had with any man. I had similar, in-depth, conversations with women I'd met while traveling, but I hadn't found the same capacity in most of the males I met.

"I'm a recovering alcoholic," he said in between talking about our spiritual journey. "I'm four years sober."

"How's that going?" I softly asked.

"Good days and bad, but even the bad days aren't a fraction of the misery I spent unconscious to the world around me." Dawes was a huge surprise. He was articulate and reflective. We continued to meet at the café every day that week. By week's end, we had packed in a lifetime of reveals. He told me that coming to Mexico was a spontaneous exit out of Nashville. He had arrived with the clothes on his back, escaping all the people in his life, that either knew or participated in his 40-year substance abuse. The pinnacle event was an Uncle that called him a '*drunk that will always be a drunk.*'

"I'll go home someday, but for now I need to find my strength, be grounded in my sobriety and be able to forgive myself.

After that first week of deep conversations over coffee, we began meeting on the outskirts of town, walking on dirt roads or in parks. We walked and talked most mornings, after I had completed my hours of writing. Some evenings, we'd meet up with Naomi and her boyfriend, Hank, for dinner and lively conversation. Dawes had told me that he had many friends, back in Tennessee, but no one in his sober-world. Hank and Dawes hit if off and seemed to bond a close friendship.

Even in our double-dating and copious time alone, Dawes hadn't attempted to make the relationship anything other than friendship, and I was grateful for that. Slowly, however, I wanted it to be more than friendship, which left me confused. I knew Perry was still in my heart and moving-on had a space of uncomfortableness Still, this man engaged something deep within and...well, my hormones.

Dawes lived in a modern one bedroom condo, on a hill overlooking the city, a 15-minute walk from town. He lived on the 6th floor and had amenities my flat was missing. Even so, we always ended up in my apartment for a meal or to relax. In late February, I invited Dawes over for a home cooked dinner (although my kitchen had limited abilities). When he arrived, I knew my heart had shifted, and I would say so. I poured us a glass of sparkling water, with a lime, and guided us to the balcony. The stars were out and soft lighting filtered up from the street.

"Dawes, I don't know if either of us is well enough for a romance, but I feel something for you that's more than friends. I'm not going to be one of those crazy ladies that tells you to feel the same or we can't..." Before I could finish the sentence, Dawes stood up, took my glass from my shaking hands, helped me stand and took me in his arms. His kiss was warm with a steady invitation. "Me, too" was all he said.

Our lovemaking was passionate and intense. I had only been with one other man my entire life, and while refusing to compare Dawes with Perry, it was undeniably different than the sex of my marriage. Dawes had endless desire and energy, and I was his muse. The next morning, I had a moment of panic that this would change our friendship and another fear that the night's passion would never happen again. Neither turned out to be true. Our walks, talks, coffee dates and lovemaking continued well into the late spring.

In March, I flew home for Franki's fifth birthday party. While I was only gone for two weeks, my return to San Miguel was met with his lavish attention. "I missed you, too much," he said our first night back together. I thought, at the time, it was a peculiar way to put that, but I shelved my concerns and enjoyed the moment. It seemed like a dream and I didn't want to wake up.

We had been a couple for five months when Dawes began to distance himself from me. It started after he had flown home to Tennessee because his mom had become ill. When he returned, he had something on his mind. While I was afraid to ask, I knew I had to. Even if I hadn't, Dawes would end up telling me. That was how we were together. In his absence, I had also begun to think about my heart and its attachment still to Perry. I didn't know how I could love both men, but I did.

"Amelia, I'm moving back home. I have more healing to do, and I need to do it there." Dawes disclosed. "It's a hard decision, but if I ignore this, my sobriety is at risk. I need to gain my strength where the weakness began." To my surprise, this announcement didn't crush me. Instead, there was a relieve that automated a heavy sigh.

"Yes, Dawes, I think you're right. I've been thinking something similar myself. It's too soon after Perry's death, and there hasn't been enough time to give this relationship the attention it deserves. I'm in a magical place, here with you, but it's not my reality. I'm going home, too. It's time". I had not actually made that decision prior to that last statement. But I knew it was the right one. It was how I functioned over the past two years; *discerning on a dime* I called it. Sometimes you just know, and not honoring what you know, can only cause regret.

Over the following week, we only saw each other twice. Both times the air was thick with genuine affection yet, mingled with the need to be elsewhere. Dawes was the first to leave, but instead of seeing him to the airport, we said our goodbye at the café where we had first met.

"Amelia, I want you to know that this wasn't a vacation-fling for me. I do deeply care for you. The timing was just off, I guess." He embraced me, and I knew he was right.

"Me, too," was all I could get out of my dry throat. Without further prolonged goodbyes, he turned and left.

The last I heard about Dawes was two years after our farewell. He was engaged to be married to a nice Tennessee girl.

In September of 2008, I returned to California and my condo I had shared with Perry.

Memories of Dawes and our love affair followed me home, still, it didn't take long to resume my life. The contents of the storage unit were easily transferred back to the condo. The stillness, however, was untenable. My night time routine was beginning to take a toll on me. I would go to bed, at a reasonable hour, but wouldn't be able to fall asleep.

In my travels, I had fallen asleep quickly and slept without issue. Now, I was back up by midnight, wandering the house, raiding the refrigerator or sitting outside and gazing at the stars.

On one such night, I removed the ancestry box from the closet shelf, and began to read Fanny's diary again. I knew I was in an *in-between place* of my life ,without a clue on what I should do next. At the same time, I knew there needed to *be* a *what's-next* plan. Winter was setting in, and I wanted to look forward to 2009, with the continued unearthing of Amelia Jane O'Malley.

I began to read from an entry dated, August 1906. They had all landed on the west coast in Canada and they were going to catch another train that would take them into Washington State. Fanny wrote about the crowds of people, all looking tired and hungry, and the struggle to find enough food each day of their journey. It must have taken them over five months to finally reach Montesano, Washington because the next entry, dated in October, indicated how rainy and cold they were, huddled under a storefront awning.

A Mrs. Caldwell spotted the family and offered them refuge in her home for the night. Later, she would help the boys find work at a local pulp-mill in Aberdeen. By the end of that first year, Fanny writes that they had a two-room shack and serious doubts about this idea of moving there.

Entry: January 1907. *Byron tok the boys to meet Mr. Brant for job. I prae for it.*

Byron? I re-read the entry. Was Byron alive? Urgently, I flipped back to the entry she had written while on the train from Ottawa.

Byron, dont die.

She hadn't said he died but that she pleaded he wouldn't. I had jumped to a conclusion, based on that conversation with Mom about Byron dying on a train.

I put the diary down on my lap and fought back the tears of my aloneness. It had been a long time since I had allowed myself to think about the death of my parents— the unthinkable suicide and mercy killing at the hands of my mother. I missed the kitchen-talks with Grandma Jane with her wisdom and love.

I wanted so desperately, at that moment, to have my great-grandmother explain how she survived such trials — to tell me what to do and to comfort me. I felt lost without Perry and even more lost having come from such adventure in my travels to ….this. The tears that I tried to squelch, fell freely down my cheeks.

A leanbh, you are stronger than you think you are, came a voice in my head. When I opened my eyes, though, there stood Grandma Jane. She was in a dress I remembered her wearing the last time I was at her home, eating Molasses cake.

"Grandma," I choked out. Tell me what to do!" I was not frightened to see her standing in my living room. Instead, I spoke as if she had never died and this was natural.

"Follow your heart, Amelia. Perry's not here anymore. He doesn't need you. You're needed elsewhere. Find out where that is, *a leanbh*".

I realized that I had not opened my eyes and the voice of Grandma Jane was from my imagination. But this is what she would have said to me, if she were still alive. She was right…or — I was right.

Where do I want to live? I dared to ask myself. *What do I want to do?*

I had read a book, while on my travels, on how to reach my creative subconsciousness. Beginning the next morning, I took out a designated notebook and trusty pen. I began the exercise of writing freestyle, in an attempt to connect to what I already knew. For two weeks, every morning, I wrote until I had nothing more to say. I didn't go back and re-read my ramblings. It was not a journal or a log of my activities. In my third week, I wrote;

I've always wanted to live near the coast. A week later I wrote, *I've always wanted to own a shop.*

On a Tuesday morning, I packed a lunch, grabbed a map and headed out toward San Francisco. I would reach Daley City and drive south, stopping as my intuition took me. Not locked on the notion to find the answer instantly, or even that day, I was relying on the process.

This *by-chance* way of living, was a clear departure from my scientific brain of outlines, graphs, and statistics. *Who had I become?* I whispered with a smile. That was what I had set out to find, for the past three years. This was just another leg of that search.

Pull off here, I thought. It was nearly 3 p.m., and I was hungry for my packed lunch. I had driven down the coast for a few hours, feeling no particular call to stop, except to get gas and look again at the map. I turned back north, heading toward home. Now, I had self- instructions to pull off the exit of Burlingame; a quiet town south of San Francisco. The downtown area of Burlingame was small and quaint.

I was drawn to drive through a small -home neighborhood just off of Main street. I liked the feel of this area, so I pulled over and got out of my car, lunch in hand. Sitting on a bench, provided in a grass and flowered round-about, I began to eat my sandwich while gazing in all directions. A brightly painted cottage caught my eye.

It was in need of repairs and tender care. The **For Sale by Owner** sign appeared weathered and I suspected had been there for a while. Gathering my lunch remains, I walked across the street and up to the house. The shades were drawn, lawn unkempt and fence to the backyard falling over in spots. Taking out my cell phone, I dialed the number on the sign. The voice that answered was raspy and soft.

"Hello," the voice greeted.

I introduced myself and said I was interested in the home she had for sale.

"Oh, good. I've been waiting for you, dear," she responded. "Come to the door. I'll be there in just a moment."

I wasn't quite sure if I wanted to see the house, now. She knew I was coming? I was a bit creeped out. But I was intuitively led to this city, this street, and now this house for reasons I didn't yet understand. Trusting my gut, I walked up to the front door and turned to view the street, expected her car to pull up to the curb. Instead, I was startled when the door opened and there stood a 5'1, woman probably in her late 80's.

"Come in, dear, please come in," she invited with a smile. As I entered, I thought of a movie I had seen as a teenager where an old woman stole children, and locked them in her basement. Gulp.

"I'm Edith Wares," she introduced with an outstretched hand.

"I'm Amelia O'Malley, pleased to meet you," I returned.

"I know, dear. Would you like some tea?" she said as she slowly turned and walked into the kitchen. Unlike the living room, that was dark with heavy draperies covering the picture window, her kitchen was bright and full of light. It overlooked a beautiful garden of flowers and bird feeders.

There was a running fountain, in the middle of the yard, with a Greek Goddess Statue, flowing water from her basket. The stark contrast of the front of the home, to this enchanting backyard view, was unbelievable. Having had my own mysterious experiences, beginning at age 12, I had to ask:

"Mrs. Wares, you said you were expecting me. How did you know? I didn't even know."

"Oh, I saw you on the bench, eating your sandwich and I saw your eyes light up when you saw my home. I knew you couldn't resist checking it out. I was right, wasn't I?" she answered.

I nodded and smiled. "Yes, you were right. But when I introduced myself you said *I know.* "

"Oh, dear, I meant I knew you were pleased to meet me. I knew you were a nice young lady with manners." At that, we both giggled, and I sat down at her kitchen table that overlooked the garden. She poured us a cup of tea in the prettiest china cup I had ever seen. She began telling me about the home she was selling. She was going to move in with her daughter, back East, because it *was all too much for an old woman to keep up.*

"I've shown the house to several nice couples, but I turned down each offer. I've been waiting for the one with that eye-sparkle I saw in you. "Do you want it, dear?" she bluntly asked.

"Yes, Mrs. Wares, I do."

The rest were detailed by the professionals, and within 45 days, Mrs. Wares had moved back East, and I had moved into 1010 Tresel Court.

As it turned out, the repairs were only cosmetic. The house was in excellent structural condition. Mrs. Wares had told me that she had deliberately kept the front looking run down so as not to attract those that didn't have a special heart for the house.

"Homes are like heartbeats, Amelia," she said at the closing. "You hear the life within, and it becomes your own."

What I didn't know then, was that this home would be my forever- home and the true heartbeat of what lied ahead.

15

Love, again

Turning 55, the year after buying the home, was uneventful as would be the next five years. *Nothing much to write home about*, as they say. I spent that time making the house my own and continuing to write my daily pages to unleash my creative life.

I finished reading Fanny's diary, too, — up to the part of the family history I already knew. The O'Malley boys started a successful lumbering business in Aberdeen, Washington. They were know as the Big Five, because each of them were over 6 feet tall! Amelia married, as did Jane — of course — and both remained in the area with Fanny. What started as tragedy for Fanny, one event after the other, settled into a quiet life for the O'Malley's. I was struck on the similarities of going through multiple tragic events, only to find myself in a life I was re-creating. *Thank you, Fanny, for carrying me through,* I said out loud while closing the tattered journal for the last time.

Still, while in the throws of actively recreating my life, I found myself lingering in limbo. In 2010, it was the email from Naomi, telling me that Dawes was engaged, that woke me back up from my lazy existence. I think I had been waiting for Dawes. I was waiting for us to continue life as a couple. The email, while painful, gave new focus to my morning pages. I realized that while once I had relied on Perry to define the path of my life, I had been doing the same in waiting for Dawes. It had been relatively unconscious, but still a driving force in my complacency.

At age 60, I followed the second of the two entry discoveries; *I've always wanted to own a shop.* A small bookstore had been for sale in the downtown square. On morning walks, I had passed it several times, musing on what it would be like to be surrounded by books.

I had no experience ordering books, creating a business plan or financial statements. I knew close to nothing about owning a business. But I knew how to research, and so I met with the Small Business Association for counsel, convinced a bank to carry a small startup loan, hired the same people from the closing bookstore and just began. If it failed, I would have learned something from that failure. If I succeeded, I would have the life I imagined.

It took two years to create the space and type of bookstore I envisioned. I added a small coffee bar and used a back storage area for both my office and space for people to gather. I intended to hold workshops on the topics that mattered to me, and I suspected mattered to others.

Burlingame was a small suburban town, but the shop was inviting and attracted locals as well as those seeking a get-away from the big city. I had hired good people to run the everyday operation of both the bistro and the book retail. I could finally concentrate on establishing the workshops and resume my writing — which would fuel the content of the training. As it turned out, I had a natural ability to sense what the bookstore needed for it to continue to grow. In the fourth year, we moved to a larger shop, three doors down on the same street.

My life was busy but quiet. I walked two blocks to work each day. I even got a cat. While I was at the bookstore 10 hours each day, I loved it. I set aside two hours, every morning, to write and four hours a day, out front running the cash register and greeting customers. Every day was slightly different but predictable enough to relax in its sweetness. By this fourth year, the business was running well enough that I even took a two-week vacation to lay on the beaches of Manzanita, Mexico.

In our fifth year open, we held a **Been In Business 5 Years** Open House. I had turned 65 just a few weeks prior but, felt like I was in my 30's. This life energized me, and I couldn't imagine a life more perfect.

The open house was in full swing, and I was in my glory, buzzing around greeting our guests and serving champaign. I recognize almost everyone there because most had been handpicked to attend. The people I didn't know, I made a point to spend time talking to. I was quite the hostess and completely in my game.

The crowds were thinning out by the end of the evening's scheduled event, and I was sitting at a table just admiring our handiwork and the success of the gala. The front doorbell sounded, as it did with each opening, and I looked up surprised that someone was coming in rather than leaving.

A tall, handsome and graying man entered the shop. It was Dawes.

Everything around me disappeared except him. My heart skipped a beat, and my eyes opened wide. I knew not to stand, because my legs wouldn't hold me. Instead, I just stared, as he crossed the room toward me.

"Hello, Amelia," he said with a large smile. "It took me a long time to find you. Don't you ever stay put?" he said in his charming southern accent.

Still speechless, he offered his hand to help me up. I hesitated only because my head was now swirling in anticipation.

I truly was questioning whether I was actually seeing Dawes or making this up — like I had seen Grandma Jane 10 years ago. His hand stayed stretched out for me to take it and I did. Standing, I faced him and finally spoke. "Do I know you?" I said breaking a smile.

"Oh, you know me," he said with a twinkle in his eye, and at that, we embraced.

It was then that I realized the staff, and those guests that had remained, were glaring with smiles of their own. I didn't want to entertain them with introductions. I could hardly recognize this moment myself, and didn't want it trivialized with social formalities. Instead, I took Dawes by the hand and guided him to the back room where we could be alone. As Dawes and I left the central shop area, I turned and instructed my staff to close up and go home. *We will clean up in the morning*, I instructed.

I had thought my life was perfect until that day. Dawe's return showed me that it *was* perfect, but it could be more than perfect. We walked back to my home that night, hand in hand, and in those short few blocks, he told me about trying to find me. He had all but given up when he received a wedding announcement from Hank, Naomi's ex-boyfriend. Dawes had lost Hank's phone number, and that was his only link to finding me. In reconnecting with Hank, he was able to locate Naomi and learn about my new life in Burlingame.

Over the next three days, we barely left the house. I had left instructions, with my staff, to *run the show* without me, but call if they needed. Dawes and I spent those days making love and talking. It had been 12 years since we had last been together, but nearly everything was the same. The only difference, now, was that we were both thoroughly ready to be together.

Dawes had now been sober for 16 years and had healed over his wounds. When I asked him about the engagement, he laughed. "Yes, well, Candice was a very nice gal, and my mom thought it was a good idea — so did I at first. It would have been the easier thing to do, but I wasn't looking for the easy way through my sobriety. The truth is, she wasn't you, Amelia."

On a warm December evening, Dawes and I married in a small intimate ceremony on Half Moon Bay. There were only 20 people present to witness our love. The twins and their wives came to represent my siblings, and one cousin on Dawes' side. Byron, Parisa and Franki came up from L.A. I had explicitly asked Carol and Kevin to attend. My wounds of my father's secret life had healed, and I wanted them to feel that resolve. The other guests were close friends and co-workers. Naomi came, and

Dawes asked her to stand with us in the ceremony because, without her help, we would never have found each other.

We honeymooned back in San Miguel, a tribute to our beginnings and grounded love. Dawes was 67, and I was 65 when we married, but we had the heart of a young couple. On our last day of the honeymoon, I was on the balcony of our hotel suite, waiting for Dawes to shower and dress. I began thinking about how far I had come from the beginning tragedies of my parent's deaths, Nathanial's dying of AIDS and Perry's heart attack. I remembered back when I cried in fear that I wouldn't be able to pay my bills or live without him. I smiled at the memories of San Ignacio, and that small studio apartment, sparse in running water. I traveled back in thought to my experiences meeting my great-grandmother and how even those times had prepared me to face the harsh stuff. All of these helped to form the person I had become.

I was not a better person now with Dawes as my husband. I had already become that *best* person. I was a mother, grandmother, business owner and now a wife again, but most of all I was Amelia. Full circle — but this time, *I* was the completed circle. I was whole.

16

2045

"I'm an old woman, Franki, telling you this story. Thank you for indulging me to tell it *like* a story not as just information for you. I know you know this, but your name is quite special. You are named after your great great great grandmother, Frances Jane O'Malley. You'll be a grandmother yourself someday soon, and you'll need to tell this story again, adding your own cross-over pieces."

"When I'm gone, Franki, I want you to have this locket and her diary. I also want you to take this letter and follow my wishes. It's my desires for burial and celebration. Your dad doesn't like to talk about my dying, so I'm asking you."

"Nana, I don't want you to go. My life's a mess and I still need you! Franki said in a tearful voice.

"Life is a mess, Franki. But there's joy as well. You just haven't been paying attention. I think that will change when you read Fanny's diary and follow my wishes. I have it, from a very reliable source. that this is true," Amelia said as she touched Franki's hand for the last time.

———

On February 14th, 2045, I, Amelia Jane O'Malley Nolan died a peaceful ending. It's like they tell you it will happen. I left my body and floated through the ceiling, watching those below as I exited. Byron, Parisa, Franki and Franki's two children were all there as I drew my last breath. I watched them cry and hold each other. It's also true that your life flashes before you, as if there's a fast-forward movie playing. I saw my birth, and all the events leading up to meeting Dawes. Then I saw my Dawes on his deathbed, just five years earlier. "I'll keep a place for you, Amelia," he kidded.

I continued to float, and then saw a lighted tunnel. Knowing this was my destined journey, I entered in without fear.

There stood Dawes, waiting for me, as he said he would. Next to him stood Grandma Jane, Nathanial, and Perry. We all embraced and together venturing further. I would later meet up with Mom and Dad, but the next person I met was Fanny.

She stood as a 12-year-old girl, in a brown dress with sunflowers at first. She took my hand and smiled. As we walked, she transformed into her adult self and put her arm around me.

"Amelia, t'is so grand to finally meet you," she said in her Irish brogue. "You know," she continued, "you saved me life that day in the waters. I wanted to die, but then I saw you and the waters turned warm, and the sun came out. I heard me Ma say she had sent you to me so I could live."

You saw me?" I asked.

"Yes, and I saw you at Da's wedding too, and at the birth of my Byron. I saw you every time and 'twas so glad I had made the decision to live. You saved me life, dear granddaughter."

How funny life is. Just when you think you have all the answers, you die and learn differently.

We walked further into the brightness. The others were slightly ahead of us leading the way. Fanny reached out to stop me. "There's one more thing for you to do for me, Amelia," she said. I waited anxiously and thinking, *What could I possibly do for her now?*

"This will probably break her heart, but I need you to tell your mother that we're not Irish. We're really Welsh."

————

Epilogue

Franki traveled to Riceville, Canada as instructed in her Nana's letter. She carried the urn in a green shopping bag and headed for a small lake, the locals told her stood on the old Blayney homestead.

Reciting the poem of her Nana's wishes, Franki began to sprinkle the ashes off of the tattered dock that ran out over the lake.

She walks in beauty, like the night

Of cloudless climes and starry skies;

And all that's best of dark and bright

Meet in her aspect and her eyes;

Thus mellowed to that tender light

Which heaven to gaudy day denies.

One shade the more, one ray the less,

Had half impaired the nameless grace

Which waves in every raven tress,

Or softly lightens o'er her face;

Where thoughts serenely sweet express,

How pure, how dear their dwelling-place.

And on that cheek, and o'er that brow,

So soft, so calm, yet eloquent,

The smiles that win, the tints that glow,

But tell of days in goodness spent,

A mind at peace with all below,

A heart whose love is innocent!

Franki had not anticipated how emotionally stirring this act would impose. She thought she had already come to terms with her Nana's death, yet releasing her in this beautiful surroundings, evoked feelings of unresolved grief and a life *less-lived*.

The tears running down her face were mixed with both sorrow, for the loss of Amelia, but also for the loss of herself. Through the years of mishaps, poor decisions, and self-abuse, Franki knew that her Nana's love had been the constant and that now, beginning that day, she would have to find a way to love herself as fiercely.

When the ashes were all released and her tears drying against her cheeks, she turned to leave and walk back toward the road where her car was parked.

Startled, Franki stopped abruptly and saw three women sitting on a large log facing the lake. They were talking and laughing, thoroughly engaged in each other's company. It was then that Franki noticed she recognized these women

The woman on the right was dressed in a pale blue ankle length dress with a white pinafore. The woman on the left was wearing a more modern slack pantsuit and casual pump-heeled shoes while the woman sitting between the two wore a house-coat she had seen in 1950 photos.

Not trusting her tear-soaked eyes, Franki blinked heavily and reopened slowly. What she was seeing was not possible but clearly there.

Her Nana, Amelia, was the younger woman sitting on the left. She recognized, from old family photos, that the one sitting between the two was Great Grandma Jane and the woman on the right was her namesake, Frances.

The women stood in unison and began to walk toward the woods, with Amelia in the lead. Franki remained standing perfectly still, mostly in disbelief , but also in fear of what was before her. Then Fanny stopped walking, and turned to look directly at Franki.

"You must carry the torch, now, Franki. Be brave and walk tall."

Stunned that this image was speaking to her, Franki remains standing like a statue. Was this the cross over experience her Nana told her about? Was she now part of this family gift? Just when she thought the experience was ending, Fanny spoke again.

"I'm not far away, Franki. You'll see me again, if you want to."

As the images of the three women, now arm in arm, fade from view, Franki laughs out loud and somehow knows she *will* see Fanny again, and that her life was about to shift in ways she could only imagine. Before turning to leave herself, she playfully mumbles under her breath,

"but first I'll need to grow out my hair!"

~The End~

About the Author

I won't write this section in third person. I'm not trying to sell you anything. You probably already have a sense that this is where you belong; reading Amelia.

So, who am I? I am a writer and crusader for women of a certain age — women in the most dynamic years of their existence — over 50. I write fiction, or what I call Synchronicity-Fiction.

We all want, at some point in our lives, to just reach for a book or audio-tape to be reassured that we are not alone in our challenges. We also want to be told how to fix it: Should I stay, or go on? Should I change careers, move, say yes to this or no to that?

The truth is, the answers are already inside of you — waiting for you to notice. The soul is shy. But once you name the discord or need, you can begin paying attention to the clues given to you. This is called synchronicities; It's the little (or big) things that show up, pointing the way.

I write about real issues women face, but I do it with fictional characters. Read the story and pay attention to what comes up for you (you will be entertained, too).

After each book, I include other resources for further exploring.

All the best,

Belle Blaney

Resources

Anderson, Joan. *A Year by the Sea*. New York: Doubletree, 2000.

Brown, Brene. *The Gifts of Imperfection*. Center City: Hazelton, 2010.

Cameron, Julia. *The Artist's Way: A Spiritual Path to Higher Creativity*. New York: Putnam, 1992.

Keirsey, David. *Please Understand Me II: Temperament, Character and Intelligence*. Del Mar: Prometheus Nemesis, 1998.

Levoy, Gregg. *Callings: Finding and Following an Authentic Life*. New York: Three Rivers Press, 1997.

Palmer, Parker. *A Hidden Wholeness: The Journey Toward an Undivided Life*. San Francisco, Jossey-Bass, 2004.

Made in the USA
San Bernardino, CA
08 June 2018